THE LEGEND OF SLEEPY HOLLOW & OTHER STORIES

MONSTROUS CLASSICS COLLECTION

Dr. Jekyll and Mr. Hyde & Other Stories
by Robert Louis Stevenson

Dracula
by Bram Stoker

Frankenstein
by Mary Shelley

The Legend of Sleepy Hollow & Other Stories
by Washington Irving

The Phantom of the Opera
by Gaston Leroux

The Raven & Other Writings
by Edgar Allan Poe

THE LEGEND OF SLEEPY HOLLOW & OTHER STORIES
MONSTROUS CLASSICS COLLECTION

BY WASHINGTON IRVING

ALADDIN
New York   Amsterdam/Antwerp   London
Toronto   Sydney/Melbourne   New Delhi

If you purchased this book without a cover, you should be aware that this book is stolen property. It was reported as "unsold and destroyed" to the publisher, and neither the author nor the publisher has received any payment for this "stripped book."

This book is a work of fiction. Any references to historical events, real people, or real places are used fictitiously. Other names, characters, places, and events are products of the author's imagination, and any resemblance to actual events or places or persons, living or dead, is entirely coincidental.

ALADDIN

An imprint of Simon & Schuster Children's Publishing Division
1230 Avenue of the Americas, New York, New York 10020
For more than 100 years, Simon & Schuster has championed authors and the stories they create. By respecting the copyright of an author's intellectual property, you enable Simon & Schuster and the author to continue publishing exceptional books for years to come. We thank you for supporting the author's copyright by purchasing an authorized edition of this book.
No amount of this book may be reproduced or stored in any format, nor may it be uploaded to any website, database, language-learning model, or other repository, retrieval, or artificial intelligence system without express permission. All rights reserved. Inquiries may be directed to Simon & Schuster, 1230 Avenue of the Americas, New York, NY 10020 or permissions@simonandschuster.com.
First Aladdin paperback edition August 2025
Text by Washington Irving
Cover illustration © 2025 by Max Kostenko
This edition includes editorial revisions.
Also available in an Aladdin hardcover edition.
All rights reserved, including the right of reproduction in whole or in part in any form.
ALADDIN and related logo are registered trademarks of Simon & Schuster, LLC.
For information about special discounts for bulk purchases, please contact Simon & Schuster Special Sales at 1-866-506-1949 or business@simonandschuster.com.
Simon & Schuster strongly believes in freedom of expression and stands against censorship in all its forms. For more information, visit BooksBelong.com.
The Simon & Schuster Speakers Bureau can bring authors to your live event. For more information or to book an event, contact the Simon & Schuster Speakers Bureau at 1-866-248-3049 or visit our website at www.simonspeakers.com.
Cover design by Irene Vandervoort based on series design by Karin Paprocki
Interior design by Mike Rosamilia
The text of this book was set in Adobe Caslon Pro.
Manufactured in the United States of America 0525 BID
2 4 6 8 10 9 7 5 3 1
Library of Congress Control Number 2024949191
ISBN 9781665974707 (hc)
ISBN 9781665974691 (pbk)
ISBN 9781665974714 (ebook)

CONTENTS

From *The Sketch Book of Geoffrey Crayon, Gent.*

The Legend of Sleepy Hollow	3
Rip Van Winkle	51
The Inn Kitchen	81
The Specter Bridegroom	85

From *Tales of a Traveller: Strange Stories by a Nervous Gentleman*

A Hunting Dinner	111
The Adventure of My Uncle	119
The Adventure of My Aunt	137
The Bold Dragoon; Or the Adventure of My Grandfather	145
The Adventure of the German Student	159
The Adventure of the Mysterious Picture	169
The Adventure of the Mysterious Stranger	183
The Story of the Young Italian	195

From *THE SKETCH BOOK OF GEOFFREY CRAYON, GENT.*

THE LEGEND OF SLEEPY HOLLOW

(Found among the Papers of the Late Diedrich Knickerbocker)

A pleasing Land of Drowsy-hed it was:
Of Dreams that wave before the half-shut Eye;
And of gay Castles in the Clouds that pass,
For ever flushing round a Summer-Sky
—*From* "The Castle of Indolence" *by James Thomson*

IN THE ENCLOSURE OF ONE OF THOSE spacious coves which indent the eastern shore of the Hudson, at that broad expansion of the river denominated by the ancient Dutch navigators the Tappan Zee, and where they always prudently shortened sail and implored the protection of Saint Nicholas when they crossed, there lies a small market town or rural port which by some is called Greensburg, but which is more generally and properly known by the name of Tarrytown. This name was given, we are told, in former days by the good housewives of the adjacent country from the inveterate propensity of their husbands to linger about the village tavern on market days. Be that as it may, I do not vouch for the fact, but merely advert to it for the sake of being precise and authentic. Not far from this village, perhaps about two miles, there is a little valley, or rather lap of land, among high hills, which is one of the quietest places in the whole world. A small brook glides through it, with just murmur enough to lull one to repose, and the occasional whistle of a quail or tapping of a woodpecker is almost the only sound that ever breaks in upon the uniform tranquility.

I recollect that when a stripling, my first exploit in squirrel-shooting was in a grove of tall walnut trees that shades one side of the valley. I had wandered into it at noontime, when all nature is peculiarly quiet, and was startled by the roar of my own gun as it broke the Sabbath stillness around and was prolonged and reverberated by the angry echoes. If ever I should wish for a retreat whither I might steal from the world and its distractions and dream quietly away the remnant of a troubled life, I know of none more promising than this little valley.

From the listless repose of the place and the peculiar character of its inhabitants, who are descendants from the original Dutch settlers, this sequestered glen has long been known by the name of Sleepy Hollow, and its rustic lads are called the Sleepy Hollow Boys throughout all the neighboring country.

A drowsy, dreamy influence seems to hang over the land and to pervade the very atmosphere. Some say that the place was bewitched by a High German doctor during the early days of the settlement; others, that an old Native American chief, the prophet or wizard of his tribe, held his powwows there before the country was claimed by Master Henry Hudson. Certain it is, the place still continues under the sway of some witching power that holds a spell over the minds of the good people, causing them to walk in a continual reverie. They are given to all kinds of marvelous beliefs, are subject to trances and visions, and frequently see strange sights and hear music and voices in the air. The whole neighborhood abounds with local tales, haunted spots, and twilight superstitions; stars shoot and meteors glare oftener across the valley than in any other part of the country, and the nightmare, with her whole ninefold, seems to make it the favorite scene of her gambols.

The dominant spirit, however, that haunts this enchanted region, and seems to be commander in chief of all the powers of the air, is the apparition of a figure on horseback without a head. It is said by some to be the ghost of a Hessian trooper whose head had been carried away by a cannonball in some nameless battle during the Revolutionary War, and who is ever and anon seen by the countryfolk hurrying along in the gloom of night as if on the wings of the wind. His haunts are not confined to the valley, but extend at times to the adjacent roads, and especially to the vicinity of a church at no great distance. Indeed, certain of the most authentic historians of those parts, who have been careful in collecting and collating the floating facts concerning this specter, allege that the body of the trooper, having been buried in the churchyard, the ghost rides forth to the scene of battle in nightly quest of his head, and that the rushing speed with which he sometimes passes along the Hollow, like a midnight blast, is owing to his being belated and in a hurry to get back to the churchyard before daybreak.

Such is the general purport of this legendary superstition, which has furnished materials for many a wild story in that region of shadows; and the specter is known at all the country firesides by the name of the Headless Horseman of Sleepy Hollow.

It is remarkable that the visionary propensity I have mentioned is not confined to the native inhabitants of the valley, but is unconsciously imbibed by everyone who resides there for a time. However wide awake they may have been before they entered that sleepy region, they are sure in a little time to inhale the witching influence of the air and begin to grow imaginative—to dream dreams and see apparitions.

I mention this peaceful spot with all possible laud, for it is in such little retired Dutch valleys, found here and there enclosed in the great state of New York, that population, manners, and customs remain fixed, while the great torrent of migration and improvement, which is making such incessant changes in other parts of this restless country, sweeps by them unobserved. They are like those little nooks of still water which border a rapid stream where we may see the straw and bubble riding quietly at anchor or slowly revolving in their mimic harbor, undisturbed by the rush of the passing current. Though many years have elapsed since I trod the drowsy shades of Sleepy Hollow, yet I question whether I should not still find the same trees and the same families vegetating in its sheltered hold.

In this by-place of nature there abode, in a remote period of American history—that is to say, some thirty years since—a worthy wight of the name of Ichabod Crane, who sojourned, or, as he expressed it, "tarried," in Sleepy Hollow for the purpose of instructing the children of the vicinity. He was a native of Connecticut, a state which supplies the Union with pioneers for the mind as well as for the forest, and sends forth yearly its legions of frontier woodmen and country schoolmasters. The cognomen of "Crane" was not inapplicable to his person. He was tall, but exceedingly lank, with narrow shoulders, long arms and legs, hands that dangled a mile out of his sleeves, feet that might have served for shovels, and his whole frame most loosely hung together. His head was small, and flat at top, with huge ears, large green glassy eyes, and a long snip nose, so that it looked like a weathervane perched upon his spindle neck to tell which way the wind blew. To see him striding along the profile of a hill on a windy day, with his clothes bagging and fluttering about him, one might have mistaken him for the genius of Famine descending upon the earth or some scarecrow eloped from a cornfield.

His schoolhouse was a low building of one large room, rudely constructed of logs, the windows partly glazed and partly patched with leaves of old copybooks. It was most ingeniously secured at vacant hours by a withe twisted in the handle of the door and stakes set against the window shutters, so that, though a thief might get in with perfect ease, he would find some embarrassment in getting out—an idea most probably borrowed by the architect, Yost Van Houten, from the mystery of an eelpot. The schoolhouse stood in a rather lonely but pleasant situation, just at the foot of a woody hill, with a brook running close by and a formidable birch tree growing at one end of it. From hence the low murmur of his pupils' voices, conning over their lessons, might be heard in a drowsy summer's day like the hum of a beehive, interrupted now and then by the authoritative voice of the master in the tone of menace or command, or, peradventure, by the appalling sound of the birch as he urged some tardy loiterer along the flowery path of knowledge. Truth to say, he was a conscientious man, and ever bore in mind the golden maxim "Spare the rod and spoil the child." Ichabod Crane's scholars certainly were not spoiled.

I would not have it imagined, however, that he was one of those cruel potentates of the school who joy in the smart of their subjects; on the contrary, he administered justice with discrimination rather than severity, taking the burden off the backs of the weak and laying it on those of the strong. Your mere puny stripling, that winced at the least flourish of the rod, was passed by with indulgence; but the claims of justice were satisfied by inflicting a double portion on some little tough, wrongheaded, broad-skirted Dutch urchin, who sulked and swelled and grew dogged and sullen beneath the birch. All this he called "doing his duty by their parents;" and he never inflicted a chastisement without following it by the assurance, so consolatory to the smarting urchin, that "he would remember it and thank him for it the longest day he had to live."

When school hours were over, he was even the companion and playmate of the larger boys, and on holiday afternoons would convoy some of the smaller ones home who happened to have pretty sisters or good housewives for mothers noted for the comforts of the cupboard. Indeed it behooved him to keep on good terms with his pupils. The revenue arising from his school was small, and would have been scarcely sufficient to furnish him with daily bread, for he was a huge feeder, and, though lank, had the dilating powers of an anaconda; but to help out his maintenance he was, according to country custom in those parts, boarded and lodged at the houses of the farmers whose children he instructed. With these he lived successively a week at a time, thus going the rounds of the neighborhood with all his worldly effects tied up in a cotton handkerchief.

That all this might not be too onerous on the purses of his rustic patrons, who are apt to consider the costs of schooling a grievous burden, and schoolmasters as mere drones, he had various ways of rendering himself both useful and agreeable. He assisted the farmers occasionally in the lighter labors of their farms, helped to make hay, mended the fences, took the horses to water, drove the cows from pasture, and cut wood for the winter fire. He laid aside, too, all the dominant dignity and absolute sway with which he lorded it in his little empire, the school, and became wonderfully gentle and ingratiating. He found favor in the eyes of the mothers by petting the children, particularly the youngest; and like the lion bold, which whilom so magnanimously the lamb did hold, he would sit with a child on one knee and rock a cradle with his foot for whole hours together.

In addition to his other vocations, he was the singing master of the neighborhood and picked up many bright shillings by instructing the young folks in psalmody. It was a matter of no little vanity to him on Sundays to take his station in front of the church gallery with a band of chosen singers, where, in his own mind, he completely carried away the palm from the parson. Certain it is, his voice resounded far above all the rest of the congregation, and there are peculiar quavers still to be heard in that church, and which may even be heard half a mile off, quite to the opposite side of the millpond on a still Sunday morning, which are said to be legitimately descended from the nose of Ichabod Crane. Thus, by divers little makeshifts in that ingenious way which is commonly denominated "by hook and by crook," the worthy pedagogue got on tolerably enough, and was thought, by all who understood nothing of the labor of headwork, to have a wonderfully easy life of it.

The schoolmaster is generally a man of some importance in the female circle of a rural neighborhood, being considered a kind of idle, gentlemanlike personage of vastly superior taste and accomplishments to the rough country swains, and, indeed, inferior in learning only to the parson. His appearance, therefore, is apt to occasion some little stir at the tea table of a farmhouse and the addition of a supernumerary dish of cakes or sweetmeats, or, peradventure, the parade of a silver teapot. Our man of letters, therefore, was peculiarly happy in the smiles of all the country damsels. How he would figure among them in the churchyard between services on Sundays, gathering grapes for them from the wild vines that overrun the surrounding trees; reciting for their amusement all the epitaphs on the tombstones; or sauntering, with a whole bevy of them, along the banks of the adjacent millpond, while the more bashful country bumpkins hung sheepishly back, envying his superior elegance and address.

From his half-itinerant life, also, he was a kind of traveling gazette, carrying the whole budget of local gossip from house to house, so that his appearance was always greeted with satisfaction. He was, moreover, esteemed by the women as a man of great erudition, for he had read several books quite through, and was a perfect master of Cotton Mather's history of New England witchcraft, in which, by the way, he most firmly and potently believed.

He was, in fact, an odd mixture of small shrewdness and simple credulity. His appetite for the marvelous and his powers of digesting it were equally extraordinary, and both had been increased by his residence in this spellbound region. No tale was too gross or monstrous for his capacious swallow. It was often his delight, after his school was dismissed in the afternoon, to stretch himself on the rich bed of clover bordering the little brook that whimpered by his schoolhouse, and there con over old Mather's direful tales until the gathering dusk of the evening made the printed page a mere mist before his eyes. Then, as he wended his way by swamp and stream and awful woodland to the farmhouse where he happened to be quartered, every sound of nature at that witching hour fluttered his excited imagination—the moan of the whip-poor-will[1] from the hillside; the boding cry of the tree toad, that harbinger of storm; the dreary hooting of the screech owl, or the sudden rustling in the thicket of birds frightened from their roost. The fireflies, too, which

---

1. The whip-poor-will is a bird which is only heard at night. It receives its name from its note, which is thought to resemble those words.

sparkled most vividly in the darkest places, now and then startled him as one of uncommon brightness would stream across his path; and if, by chance, a huge blockhead of a beetle came winging his blundering flight against him, the poor varlet was ready to give up the ghost, with the idea that he was struck with a witch's token. His only resource on such occasions, either to drown thought or drive away evil spirits, was to sing psalm tunes; and the good people of Sleepy Hollow, as they sat by their doors of an evening, were often filled with awe at hearing his nasal melody, "in linked sweetness long drawn out," floating from the distant hill or along the dusky road.

Another of his sources of fearful pleasure was to pass long winter evenings with the old Dutch wives as they sat spinning by the fire, with a row of apples roasting and spluttering along the hearth, and listen to their marvelous tales of ghosts and goblins, and haunted fields, and haunted brooks, and haunted bridges, and haunted houses, and particularly of the headless horseman, or Galloping Hessian of the Hollow, as they sometimes called him. He would delight them equally by his anecdotes of witchcraft and of the direful omens and portentous sights and sounds in the air which prevailed in the earlier times of Connecticut, and would frighten them woefully with speculations upon comets and shooting stars, and with the alarming fact that the world did absolutely turn round and that they were half the time topsy-turvy.

But if there was a pleasure in all this while snugly cuddling in the chimney corner of a chamber that was all of a ruddy glow from the crackling wood fire, and where, of course, no specter dared to show its face, it was dearly purchased by the terrors of his subsequent walk homewards. What fearful shapes and shadows beset his path amidst the dim and ghastly glare of a snowy night! With what wistful look did he eye every trembling ray of light streaming across the waste fields from some distant window! How often was he appalled by some shrub covered with snow, which, like a sheeted specter, beset his very path! How often did he shrink with curdling awe at the sound of his own steps on the frosty crust beneath his feet, and dread to look over his shoulder, lest he should behold some uncouth being tramping close behind him! And how often was he thrown into complete dismay by some rushing blast howling among the trees, in the idea that it was the Galloping Hessian on one of his nightly scourings!

All these, however, were mere terrors of the night, phantoms of the mind that walk in darkness; and though he had seen many specters in his time, and been more than once beset by Satan in divers shapes in his lonely perambulations, yet daylight put an end to all these evils; and he would have passed a pleasant life of it, in despite of the devil and all his works, if his path had not been crossed by a being that causes more perplexity to mortal man than ghosts, goblins, and the whole race of witches put together, and that was—a woman.

Among the musical disciples who assembled one evening in each week to receive his instructions in psalmody was Katrina Van Tassel, the daughter and only child of a substantial Dutch farmer. She was a blooming lass of fresh eighteen, as plump as a partridge, as ripe and melting and rosy-cheeked as one of her father's peaches, and universally famed, not merely for her beauty but her vast expectations. She was withal a little coy, as might be perceived even in her dress, which was a mixture of ancient and modern fashions, as most suited to set off her charms. She wore the ornaments of pure yellow gold which her great-great-grandmother had brought over from Zaandam, the tempting stomacher of the olden time, and withal a provokingly short petticoat to display the prettiest foot and ankle in the country round.

Ichabod Crane had a soft and foolish heart towards the sex, and it is not to be wondered at that so tempting a morsel soon found favor in his eyes, more especially after he had visited her in her paternal mansion. Old Baltus Van Tassel was a perfect picture of a thriving, contented, liberal-hearted farmer. He seldom, it is true, sent either his eyes or his thoughts beyond the boundaries of his own farm, but within those everything was snug, happy, and well-conditioned. He was satisfied with his wealth but not proud of it, and piqued himself upon the hearty abundance, rather than the style, in which he lived. His stronghold was situated on the banks of the Hudson, in one of those green, sheltered, fertile nooks in which the Dutch farmers are so fond of nestling. A great elm tree spread its broad branches over it, at the foot of which bubbled up a spring of the softest and sweetest water in a little well, formed of a barrel, and then stole sparkling away through the grass to a neighboring brook that bubbled along among alders and dwarf willows. Hard by the farmhouse was a vast barn, that might have served for a church, every window and crevice of which seemed bursting forth with the treasures of the farm; the flail was busily resounding within it from morning to night; swallows and martins skimmed twittering about the eaves; and rows of pigeons, some with one eye turned up, as if watching the weather, some with their heads under their wings or buried in their chests, and others, swelling, and cooing, and bowing about their dames, were enjoying the sunshine on the roof. Sleek, unwieldy porkers were grunting in the repose and abundance of their pens, whence sallied forth, now and then, troops of sucking pigs as if to snuff the air. A stately squadron of snowy geese were riding in an adjoining pond, convoying whole fleets of ducks; regiments of turkeys were gobbling through the farmyard, and guinea-fowls fretting about it, like ill-tempered housewives, with their peevish, discontented cry. Before the barn door strutted the gallant rooster that pattern of a husband, a warrior, and a fine gentleman, clapping his burnished wings and crowing in the pride and gladness of his heart—sometimes tearing up the earth with his feet, and then generously calling his ever-hungry family of wives and children to enjoy the rich morsel which he had discovered.

The pedagogue's mouth watered as he looked upon this sumptuous promise of luxurious winter fare. In his devouring mind's eye he pictured to himself every roasting pig running about with a pudding in his belly and an apple in his mouth; the pigeons were snugly put to bed in a comfortable pie and tucked in with a coverlet of crust; the geese were swimming in their own gravy; and the ducks pairing cozily in dishes, like snug married couples, with a decent competency of onion sauce. In the porkers he saw carved out the future sleek side of bacon and juicy relishing ham; not a turkey but he beheld daintily trussed up, with its gizzard under its wing, and, peradventure, a necklace of savory sausages; and even bright chanticleer himself lay sprawling on his back in a side dish, with uplifted claws, as if craving that quarter which his chivalrous spirit disdained to ask while living.

As the enraptured Ichabod fancied all this, and as he rolled his great green eyes over the fat meadowlands, the rich fields of wheat, of rye, of buckwheat, and corn, and the orchards burdened with ruddy fruit, which surrounded the warm tenement of Van Tassel, his heart yearned after the damsel who was to inherit these domains, and his imagination expanded with the idea how thedy might be readily turned into cash and the money invested in immense tracts of wild land and shingle palaces in the wilderness. Nay, his busy fancy already realized his hopes, and presented to him the blooming

Katrina, with a whole family of children, mounted on the top of a wagon loaded with household trumpery, with pots and kettles dangling beneath, and he beheld himself bestriding a pacing mare, with a colt at her heels, setting out for Kentucky, Tennessee, or the Lord knows where.

When he entered the house, the conquest of his heart was complete. It was one of those spacious farmhouses with high-ridged but lowly sloping roofs, built in the style handed down from the first Dutch settlers, the low projecting eaves forming a piazza along the front capable of being closed up in bad weather. Under this were hung flails, harness, various utensils of husbandry, and nets for fishing in the neighboring river. Benches were built along the sides for summer use, and a great spinning wheel at one end and a churn at the other showed the various uses to which this important porch might be devoted. From this piazza the wondering Ichabod entered the hall, which formed the center of the mansion and the place of usual residence. Here rows of resplendent pewter, ranged on a long dresser, dazzled his eyes. In one corner stood a huge bag of wool ready to be spun; in another a quantity of linsey-woolsey just from the loom; ears of corn and strings of dried apples and peaches hung in joyous festoons along the walls, mingled with the gaud of red peppers; and a door left ajar gave him a peep into the best parlor, where the claw-footed chairs and dark mahogany tables shone like mirrors; andirons, with their accompanying shovel and tongs, glistened from their covert of asparagus tops; mock oranges and conch shells decorated the mantelpiece; strings of various-colored birds' eggs were suspended above it; a great ostrich egg was hung from the center of the room, and a corner cupboard, knowingly left open, displayed immense treasures of old silver and well-mended china.

From the moment Ichabod laid his eyes upon these regions of delight, the peace of his mind was at an end, and his only study was how to gain the affections of the peerless daughter of Van Tassel. In this enterprise, however, he had more real difficulties than generally fell to the lot of a knight-errant of yore, who seldom had anything but giants, enchanters, fiery dragons, and suchlike easily conquered adversaries to contend with, and had to make his way merely through gates of iron and brass and walls of adamant to the castle keep, where the lady of his heart was confined; all which he achieved as easily as a man would carve his way to the center of a Christmas pie, and then the lady gave him her hand as a matter of course. Ichabod, on the contrary, had to win his way to the heart of a country woman beset with a labyrinth of whims and caprices, which were forever presenting new difficulties and impediments, and he had to encounter a host of fearful adversaries of real flesh and blood, the numerous rustic admirers who beset every portal to her heart, keeping a watchful and angry eye upon each other, but ready to fly out in the common cause against any new competitor.

Among these the most formidable was a burly, roaring,

roistering blade of the name of Abraham—or, according to the Dutch abbreviation, Brom—Van Brunt, the hero of the country round, which rang with his feats of strength and hardihood. He was broad-shouldered and double-jointed, with short curly black hair and a bluff but not unpleasant countenance, having a mingled air of fun and arrogance. From his Herculean frame and great powers of limb, he had received the nickname of Brom Bones, by which he was universally known. He was famed for great knowledge and skill in horsemanship, being as dexterous on horseback as a Tartar. He was foremost at all races and rooster fights, and, with the ascendancy which bodily strength acquires in rustic life, was the umpire in all disputes, setting his hat on one side and giving his decisions with an air and tone admitting of no gainsay or appeal. He was always ready for either a fight or a frolic, but had more mischief than ill will in his composition; and with all his overbearing roughness there was a strong dash of waggish good humor at bottom. He had three or four boon companions who regarded him as their model, and at the head of whom he scoured the country, attending every scene of feud or merriment for miles around. In cold weather he was distinguished by a fur cap surmounted with a flaunting fox's tail; and when the folks at a country gathering descried this well-known crest at a distance, whisking about among a squad of hard riders, they always stood by for a squall. Sometimes his crew would be heard dashing along past the farmhouses at midnight with whoop and halloo, like a troop of Don Cossacks, and the old dames, startled out of their sleep, would listen for a moment till the hurry-scurry had clattered by, and then exclaim, "Ay, there goes Brom Bones and his gang!" The neighbors looked upon him with a mixture of awe, admiration, and goodwill, and when any madcap prank or rustic brawl occurred in the vicinity always shook their heads and warranted Brom Bones was at the bottom of it.

This rantipole hero had for some time singled out the blooming Katrina for the object of his uncouth gallantries, and, though his amorous toyings were something like the gentle caresses and endearments of a bear, yet it was whispered that she did not altogether discourage his hopes. Certain it is, his advances were signals for rival candidates to retire who felt no inclination to cross a line in his amours; insomuch that, when his horse was seen tied to Van Tassel's paling on a Sunday night, a sure sign that his master was courting—or, as it is termed, "sparking"—within, all other suitors passed by in despair and carried the war into other quarters.

Such was the formidable rival with whom Ichabod Crane had to contend, and, considering all things, a stouter man than he would have shrunk from the competition, and a wiser man would have despaired. He had, however, a happy mixture of pliability and perseverance in his nature; he was in form and spirit like a supple jack—yielding, but tough; though he bent, he never broke, and though he bowed beneath the slightest pressure, yet the moment it was away, jerk! he was as erect and carried his head as high as ever.

To have taken the field openly against his rival would have been madness, for he was not a man to be thwarted in his amours, any more than that stormy lover Achilles. Ichabod, therefore, made his advances in a quiet and gently insinuating manner. Under cover of his character of singing master, he made frequent visits at the farmhouse; not that he had anything to apprehend from the meddlesome interference of parents, which is so often a stumbling block in the path of lovers. Balt Van Tassel was an easy, indulgent soul; he loved his daughter better even than his pipe, and, like a reasonable man and an excellent father, let her have her way in everything. His notable little wife, too, had enough to do to attend to her housekeeping and manage her poultry, for, as she sagely observed, ducks and geese are foolish things and must be looked after, but girls can take care of themselves. Thus while the busy dame bustled about the house or plied her spinning wheel at one end of the piazza, honest Balt would sit smoking his evening pipe at the other, watching the achievements of a little wooden warrior who, armed with a sword in each hand, was most valiantly fighting the wind on the pinnacle of the barn. In the meantime, Ichabod would carry on his suit with the daughter by the side of the spring under the great elm, or sauntering along in the twilight, that hour so favorable to the lover's eloquence.

I profess not to know how women's hearts are wooed and won. To me they have always been matters of riddle and admiration. Some seem to have but one vulnerable point, or door of access, while others have a thousand avenues and may be captured in a thousand different ways. It is a great triumph of skill to gain the former, but still greater proof of generalship to maintain possession of the latter, for the man must battle for his fortress at every door and window. He who wins a thousand common hearts is therefore entitled to some renown, but he who keeps undisputed sway over the heart of a coquette is indeed a hero. Certain it is, this was not the case with the redoubtable Brom Bones; and from the moment Ichabod Crane made his advances, the interests of the former evidently declined; his horse was no longer seen tied at the palings on Sunday nights, and a deadly feud gradually arose between him and the preceptor of Sleepy Hollow.

Brom, who had a degree of rough chivalry in his nature, would fain have carried matters to open warfare, and have settled their pretensions to the lady according to the mode of those most concise and simple reasoners, the knights-errant of yore—by single combat; but Ichabod was too conscious of the superior might of his adversary to enter the lists against him: he had overheard a boast of Bones, that he would "double the schoolmaster up and lay him on a shelf of his own schoolhouse;" and he was too wary to give him an opportunity. There was something extremely provoking in this obstinately pacific system; it left Brom no alternative but to draw upon the funds of rustic waggery in his disposition and to play off boorish practical jokes upon his rival. Ichabod became the object of whimsical persecution to Bones and his gang of rough riders. They harried his hitherto peaceful domains; smoked out his singing school by stopping up the chimney; broke into the schoolhouse at night in spite of its formidable fastenings of withe and window stakes, and turned everything topsy-turvy; so that the poor schoolmaster began to think all the witches in the country held their meetings there. But, what was still more annoying, Brom took all opportunities of turning him into ridicule in presence of his mistress, and had a scoundrel dog whom he taught to whine in the most ludicrous manner, and introduced as a rival of Ichabod's, to instruct her in psalmody.

In this way, matters went on for some time without producing any material effect on the relative situation of the contending powers. On a fine autumnal afternoon Ichabod, in pensive mood, sat enthroned on the lofty stool whence he usually watched all the concerns of his little literary realm. In his hand he swayed a ferule, that scepter of despotic power; the birch of justice reposed on three nails behind the throne, a constant terror to evildoers; while on the desk before him might be seen sundry contraband articles and prohibited weapons detected upon the persons of idle urchins, such as half-munched apples, popguns, whirligigs, fly-cages, and whole legions of rampant little paper roosters. Apparently there had been some appalling act of justice recently inflicted, for his scholars were all busily intent upon their books or slyly whispering behind them with one eye kept upon the master, and a kind of buzzing stillness reigned throughout the schoolroom. It was suddenly interrupted by the appearance of an African American man in tow-cloth jacket and trousers, a round-crowned fragment of a hat like the cap of Mercury, and mounted on the back of a ragged, wild, half-broken colt, which he managed with a rope by way of halter. He came clattering up to the school door with an invitation to Ichabod to attend a merrymaking or "quilting frolic" to be held that evening at Mynheer Van Tassel's; and, having delivered his message with that air of importance and effort at fine language which an African American is apt to display on petty embassies of the kind, he dashed over the brook, and was seen scampering away up the hollow, full of the importance and hurry of his mission.

All was now bustle and hubbub in the late quiet schoolroom. The scholars were hurried through their lessons without stopping at trifles; those who were nimble skipped over half with impunity, and those who were tardy had a smart application now and then in the rear to quicken their speed or help them over a tall word. Books were flung aside without being put away on the shelves, inkstands were overturned, benches thrown down, and the whole school was turned loose an hour before the usual time, bursting forth like a legion of young imps, yelping and racketing about the green in joy at their early emancipation.

The gallant Ichabod now spent at least an extra half hour at his toilet, brushing and furbishing up his best, and indeed only, suit of rusty black, and arranging his locks by a bit of broken looking glass that hung up in the schoolhouse. That he might make his appearance before his mistress in the true style of a cavalier, he borrowed a horse from the farmer with whom he was domiciliated, a choleric old Dutchman of the name of Hans Van Ripper, and, thus gallantly mounted, issued forth like a knight-errant in quest of adventures. But it is meet I should, in the true spirit of romantic story, give some account of the looks and equipments of my hero and his steed. The animal he bestrode was a broken-down plow horse that had outlived almost everything but his viciousness. He was gaunt and shagged, with a ewe neck and a head like a hammer; his rusty mane and tail were tangled and knotted with burrs; one eye had lost its pupil and was glaring and spectral, but the other had the gleam of a genuine devil in it. Still, he must have had fire and mettle in his day, if we may judge from the name he bore of Gunpowder. He had, in fact, been a favorite steed of his master's, the choleric Van Ripper, who was a furious rider, and had infused, very probably, some of his own spirit into the animal; for, old and broken-down as he looked, there was more of the lurking devil in him than in any young filly in the country.

Ichabod was a suitable figure for such a steed. He rode with short stirrups, which brought his knees nearly up to the pommel of the saddle; his sharp elbows stuck out like grasshoppers'; he carried his whip perpendicularly in his hand like a scepter; and as his horse jogged on, the motion of his arms was not unlike the flapping of a pair of wings. A small wool hat rested on the top of his nose, for so his scanty strip of forehead might be called, and the skirts of his black coat fluttered out almost to his horse's tail. Such was the appearance of Ichabod and his steed as they shambled out of the gate of Hans Van Ripper, and it was altogether such an apparition as is seldom to be met with in broad daylight.

It was, as I have said, a fine autumnal day; the sky was clear and serene, and nature wore that rich and golden livery which we always associate with the idea of abundance. The forests had put on their sober brown and yellow, while some trees of the tenderer kind had been nipped by the frosts into brilliant dyes of orange, purple, and scarlet. Streaming files of wild ducks began to make their appearance high in the air; the bark of the squirrel might be heard from the groves of beech and hickory nuts, and the pensive whistle of the quail at intervals from the neighboring stubble field.

The small birds were taking their farewell banquets. In the fullness of their revelry they fluttered, chirping and frolicking, from bush to bush and tree to tree, capricious from the very profusion and variety around them. There was the honest robin, the favorite game of stripling sportsmen, with its loud querulous note; and the twittering blackbirds, flying in sable clouds; and the golden-winged woodpecker, with his crimson crest, his broad black gorget, and splendid plumage; and the cedarbird, with its red-tipped wings and yellow-tipped tail and its little montero cap of feathers; and the blue jay, that noisy coxcomb, in his joyful light-blue coat and white underclothes, screaming and chattering, bobbing and nodding and bowing, and pretending to be on good terms with every songster of the grove.

As Ichabod jogged slowly on his way, his eye, ever open to every symptom of culinary abundance, ranged with delight over the treasures of jolly autumn. On all sides he beheld vast stores of apples—some hanging in oppressive opulence on the trees, some gathered into baskets and barrels for the market, others heaped up in rich piles for the cider press. Farther on he beheld great fields of corn, with its golden ears peeping from their leafy coverts and holding out the promise of cakes and hasty pudding; and the yellow pumpkins lying beneath them, turning up their fair round bellies to the sun, and giving ample prospects of the most luxurious of pies; and anon he passed the fragrant buckwheat fields, breathing the odor of the beehive, and as he beheld them, soft anticipations stole over his mind of dainty slapjacks, well buttered and garnished with honey or treacle by the delicate little dimpled hand of Katrina Van Tassel.

Thus feeding his mind with many sweet thoughts and

"sugared suppositions," he journeyed along the sides of a range of hills which look out upon some of the goodliest scenes of the mighty Hudson. The sun gradually wheeled his broad disk down into the west. The wide chest of the Tappan Zee lay motionless and glassy, excepting that here and there a gentle undulation waved and prolonged the blue shadow of the distant mountain. A few amber clouds floated in the sky, without a breath of air to move them. The horizon was of a fine golden tint, changing gradually into a pure apple green, and from that into the deep blue of the midheaven. A slanting ray lingered on the woody crests of the precipices that overhung some parts of the river, giving greater depth to the dark-gray and purple of their rocky sides. A sloop was loitering in the distance, dropping slowly down with the tide, her sail hanging uselessly against the mast, and as the reflection of the sky gleamed along the still water, it seemed as if the vessel was suspended in the air.

It was toward evening that Ichabod arrived at the castle of the Heer Van Tassel, which he found thronged with the pride and flower of the adjacent country—old farmers, a spare leather-faced race, in homespun coats and breeches, blue stockings, huge shoes, and magnificent pewter buckles; their brisk withered little dames, in close crimped caps, long-waisted short gowns, homespun petticoats, with scissors and pincushions and festive calico pockets hanging on the outside; buxom lasses, almost as antiquated as their mothers, excepting where a straw hat, a fine ribbon, or perhaps a white frock, gave symptoms of city innovation; the sons, in short square-skirted coats with rows of stupendous brass buttons, and their hair generally queued in the fashion of the times, especially if they could procure an eel skin for the purpose, it being esteemed throughout the country as a potent nourisher and strengthener of the hair.

Brom Bones, however, was the hero of the scene, having come to the gathering on his favorite steed, Daredevil—a creature, like himself, full of metal and mischief, and which no one but himself could manage. Brom was, in fact, noted for preferring vicious animals, given to all kinds of tricks, which kept the rider in constant risk of his neck, for he held a tractable, well-broken horse as unworthy of a lad of spirit.

Fain would I pause to dwell upon the world of charms that burst upon the enraptured gaze of my hero as he entered the state parlor of Van Tassel's mansion. Not those of the bevy of buxom lasses with their luxurious display of red and white, but the ample charms of a genuine Dutch country tea table in the sumptuous time of autumn. Such heaped-up platters of cakes of various and almost indescribable kinds, known only to experienced Dutch housewives! There was the doughty doughnut, the tenderer oily koek, and the crisp and crumbling cruller; sweet cakes and short cakes, ginger cakes and honey cakes, and the whole family of cakes. And then there were apple pies and peach pies and pumpkin pies; besides slices of ham and smoked beef; and moreover delectable dishes of preserved plums and peaches and pears and quinces; not to mention broiled shad and roasted chickens; together with bowls of milk and cream—all mingled higgledy-piggledy, pretty much as I have enumerated them, with the motherly teapot sending up its clouds of vapor from the midst. Heaven bless the mark! I want breath and time to discuss this banquet as it deserves, and am too eager to get on with my story. Happily, Ichabod Crane was not in so great a hurry as his historian, but did ample justice to every dainty.

He was a kind and thankful creature, whose heart dilated in proportion as his skin was filled with good cheer, and whose spirits rose with eating as some men's do with drink. He could not help, too, rolling his large eyes round him as he ate, and chuckling with the possibility that he might one day be lord of all this scene of almost unimaginable luxury and splendor. Then, he thought, how soon he'd turn his back upon the old schoolhouse, snap his fingers in the face of Hans Van Ripper and every other patron, and kick any itinerant pedagogue out of doors that should dare to call him comrade!

Old Baltus Van Tassel moved about among his guests with a face dilated with content and good humor, as round and jolly as the harvest moon. His hospitable attentions were brief, but expressive, being confined to a shake of the hand, a slap on the shoulder, a loud laugh, and a pressing invitation to "fall to and help themselves."

And now the sound of the music from the common room, or hall, summoned to the dance. The musician was an old gray-headed African American man who had been the itinerant orchestra of the neighborhood for more than half a century. His instrument was as old and battered as himself. The greater part of the time he scraped on two or three strings, accompanying every movement of the bow with a motion of the head, bowing almost to the ground and stamping with his foot whenever a fresh couple were to start.

Ichabod prided himself upon his dancing as much as upon his vocal powers. Not a limb, not a fiber about him was idle; and to have seen his loosely hung frame in full motion and clattering about the room you would have thought Saint Vitus himself, that blessed patron of the dance, was figuring before you in person. He was the admiration of all the men, who, having gathered, of all ages and sizes, from the farm and the neighborhood, stood forming a pyramid of shining faces at every door and window, gazing with delight at the scene, rolling their white eyeballs, and showing grinning rows of ivory from ear to ear. How could the flogger of urchins be otherwise than animated and joyous? The lady of his heart was his partner in the dance, and smiling graciously in reply to all his amorous oglings, while Brom Bones, sorely smitten with love and jealousy, sat brooding by himself in one corner.

When the dance was at an end, Ichabod was attracted to a knot of the sager folks, who, with old Van Tassel, sat smoking at one end of the piazza, gossiping over former times and drawing out long stories about the war.

This neighborhood, at the time of which I am speaking, was one of those highly favored places which abound with chronicle and great men. The British and American line had run near it during the war; it had therefore been the scene of marauding and infested with refugees, cowboys, and all kinds of border chivalry. Just sufficient time had elapsed to enable each storyteller to dress up his tale with a little becoming fiction, and in the indistinctness of his recollection to make himself the hero of every exploit.

There was the story of Doffue Martling, a large blue-bearded Dutchman, who had nearly taken a British frigate with an old iron nine-pounder from a mud breastwork, only that his gun burst at the sixth discharge. And there was an old gentleman who shall be nameless, being too rich a mynheer to be lightly mentioned, who, in the Battle of White Plains, being an excellent master of defense, parried a musket ball with a small sword, insomuch that he absolutely felt it whiz round the blade and glance off at the hilt: in proof of which he was ready at any time to show the sword, with the hilt a little bent. There were several more that had been equally great in the field, not one of whom but was persuaded that he had a considerable hand in bringing the war to a happy termination.

But all these were nothing to the tales of ghosts and

apparitions that succeeded. The neighborhood is rich in legendary treasures of the kind. Local tales and superstitions thrive best in these sheltered, long-settled retreats but are trampled underfoot by the shifting throng that forms the population of most of our country places. Besides, there is no encouragement for ghosts in most of our villages, for they have scarcely had time to finish their first nap and turn themselves in their graves before their surviving friends have traveled away from the neighborhood; so that when they turn out at night to walk their rounds, they have no acquaintance left to call upon. This is perhaps the reason why we so seldom hear of ghosts except in our long-established Dutch communities.

The immediate causes however, of the prevalence of supernatural stories in these parts, was doubtless owing to the vicinity of Sleepy Hollow. There was a contagion in the very air that blew from that haunted region; it breathed forth an atmosphere of dreams and fancies infecting all the land. Several of the Sleepy Hollow people were present at Van Tassel's, and, as usual, were doling out their wild and wonderful legends. Many dismal tales were told about funeral trains and mourning cries and wailings heard and seen about the great tree where the unfortunate Major Andre was taken, and which stood in the neighborhood. Some mention was made also of the woman in white that haunted the dark glen at Raven Rock, and was often heard to shriek on winter nights before a storm, having perished there in the snow. The chief part of the stories, however, turned upon the favorite specter of Sleepy Hollow, the headless horseman, who had been heard several times of late patrolling the country, and, it was said, tethered his horse nightly among the graves in the churchyard.

The sequestered situation of this church seems always to have made it a favorite haunt of troubled spirits. It stands on a knoll surrounded by locust trees and lofty elms, from among which its decent whitewashed walls shine modestly forth, like Christian purity beaming through the shades of retirement. A gentle slope descends from it to a silver sheet of water bordered by high trees, between which peeps may be caught at the blue hills of the Hudson. To look upon its grass-grown yard, where the sunbeams seem to sleep so quietly, one would think that there at least the dead might rest in peace. On one side of the church extends a wide woody dell, along which raves a large brook among broken rocks and trunks of fallen trees. Over a deep black part of the stream, not far from the church, was formerly thrown a wooden bridge; the road that led to it and the bridge itself were thickly shaded by overhanging trees, which cast a gloom about it even in the daytime, but occasioned a fearful darkness at night. Such was one of the favorite haunts of the headless horseman, and the place where he was most frequently encountered. The tale was told of old Brouwer, a most heretical disbeliever in ghosts, how he met the horseman returning from his foray into Sleepy Hollow, and was obliged to get up behind him;

how they galloped over bush and brake, over hill and swamp, until they reached the bridge, when the horseman suddenly turned into a skeleton, threw old Brouwer into the brook, and sprang away over the treetops with a clap of thunder.

This story was immediately matched by a thrice-marvelous adventure of Brom Bones, who made light of the galloping Hessian as an arrant jockey. He affirmed that on returning one night from the neighboring village of Sing-Sing, he had been overtaken by this midnight trooper; that he had offered to race with him for a bowl of punch, and should have won it too, for Daredevil beat the goblin horse all hollow, but just as they came to the church bridge, the Hessian bolted and vanished in a flash of fire.

All these tales, told in that drowsy undertone with which men talk in the dark, the countenances of the listeners only now and then receiving a casual gleam from the glare of a pipe, sank deep into the mind of Ichabod. He repaid them in kind with large extracts from his invaluable author, Cotton Mather, and added many marvelous events that had taken place in his native state of Connecticut and fearful sights which he had seen in his nightly walks about Sleepy Hollow.

The revel now gradually broke up. The old farmers gathered together their families in their wagons, and were heard for some time rattling along the hollow roads and over the distant hills. Some of the damsels mounted on pillions behind their favorite swains, and their lighthearted laughter, mingling with the clatter of hoofs, echoed along the silent woodlands, sounding fainter and fainter until they gradually died away, and the late scene of noise and frolic was all silent and deserted. Ichabod only lingered behind, according to the custom of country lovers, to have a tête-à-tête with the heiress, fully convinced that he was now on the high road to success. What passed at this interview I will not pretend to say, for in fact I do not know. Something, however, I fear me, must have gone wrong, for he certainly sallied forth, after no very great interval, with an air quite desolate and chopfallen. Oh these women! These women! Could that girl have been playing off any of her coquettish tricks? Was her encouragement of the poor pedagogue all a mere sham to secure her conquest of his rival? Heaven only knows, not I! Let it suffice to say, Ichabod stole forth with the air of one who had been sacking a henroost, rather than a fair lady's heart. Without looking to the right or left to notice the scene of rural wealth on which he had so often gloated, he went straight to the stable, and with several hearty cuffs and kicks roused his steed most uncourteously from the comfortable quarters in which he was soundly sleeping, dreaming of mountains of corn and oats and whole valleys of timothy and clover.

It was the very witching time of night that Ichabod, heavyhearted and crestfallen, pursued his travel homewards along the sides of the lofty hills which rise above Tarrytown, and which he had traversed so cheerily in the afternoon. The hour was as dismal as himself. Far below him the Tappan Zee spread its dusky and indistinct waste of waters, with here and there the tall mast of a sloop riding quietly at anchor under the land. In the dead hush of midnight he could even hear the barking of the watchdog from the opposite shore of the Hudson; but it was so vague and faint as only to give an idea of his distance from this faithful companion of man. Now and then, too, the long-drawn crowing of a rooster, accidentally awakened, would sound far, far off, from some farmhouse away among the hills; but it was like a dreaming sound in his ear. No signs of life occurred near him, but occasionally the melancholy chirp of a cricket, or perhaps the guttural twang of a bullfrog from a neighboring marsh, as if sleeping uncomfortably and turning suddenly in his bed.

All the stories of ghosts and goblins that he had heard in the afternoon now came crowding upon his recollection. The night grew darker and darker; the stars seemed to sink deeper in the sky, and driving clouds occasionally had them from his sight. He had never felt so lonely and dismal. He was, moreover, approaching the very place where many of the scenes of the ghost stories had been laid. In the center of the road stood an enormous tulip tree which towered like a giant above all the other trees of the neighborhood and formed a kind of landmark. Its limbs were gnarled and fantastic, large enough to form trunks for ordinary trees, twisting down almost to the earth and rising again into the air. It was connected with the tragical story of the unfortunate Andre, who had been taken prisoner hard by, and was universally known by the name of Major Andre's tree. The common people regarded it with a mixture of respect and superstition, partly out of sympathy for the fate of its ill-starred namesake, and partly from the tales of strange sights and doleful lamentations told concerning it.

As Ichabod approached this fearful tree, he began to whistle; he thought his whistle was answered; it was but a blast sweeping sharply through the dry branches. As he approached a little nearer, he thought he saw something white hanging in the midst of the tree; he paused and ceased whistling, but on looking more narrowly perceived that it was a place where the tree had been scathed by lightning and the white wood laid bare. Suddenly he heard a groan; his teeth chattered and his knees smote against the saddle; it was but the rubbing of one huge bough upon another as they were swayed about by the breeze. He passed the tree in safety, but new perils lay before him.

About two hundred yards from the tree, a small brook crossed the road and ran into a marshy and thickly wooded glen known by the name of Wiley's Swamp. A few rough logs, laid side by side, served for a bridge over this stream. On that side of the road where the brook entered the wood a group of oaks and chestnuts, matted thick with wild grapevines, threw a cavernous gloom over it. To pass this bridge was the severest trial. It was at this identical spot that the unfortunate Andre was captured, and under the covert of those chestnuts and vines were the sturdy yeomen concealed who surprised him. This has ever since been considered a haunted stream, and fearful are the feelings of the schoolboy who has to pass it alone after dark.

As Ichabod approached the stream, his heart began to thump; he summoned up, however, all his resolution, gave his horse half a score of kicks in the ribs, and attempted to dash briskly across the bridge; but instead of starting forward, the perverse old animal made a lateral movement and ran broadside against the fence. Ichabod, whose fears increased with the delay, jerked the reins on the other side and kicked lustily with the contrary foot; it was all in vain; his steed started, it is true, but it was only to plunge to the opposite side of the road into a thicket of brambles and alder bushes. The schoolmaster now bestowed both whip and heel upon the starveling ribs of old Gunpowder, who dashed forward, snuffing and snorting, but came to a stand just by the bridge with a suddenness that had nearly sent his rider sprawling over his head. Just at this moment a plashy stomp by the side of the bridge caught the sensitive ear of Ichabod. In the dark shadow of the grove on the margin of the brook he beheld something huge, misshapen, black, and towering. It stirred not, but seemed gathered up in the gloom, like some gigantic monster ready to spring upon the traveler.

The hair of the affrighted pedagogue rose upon his head with terror. What was to be done? To turn and fly was now too late; and besides, what chance was there of escaping ghost or goblin, if such it was, which could ride upon the wings of the wind? Summoning up, therefore, a show of courage, he demanded in stammering accents, "Who are you?" He received no reply. He repeated his demand in a still more agitated voice. Still there was no answer. Once more he cudgeled the sides of the inflexible Gunpowder, and, shutting his eyes, broke forth with involuntary fervor into a psalm tune. Just then the shadowy object of alarm put itself in motion, and with a scramble and a bound stood at once in the middle of the road. Though the night was dark and dismal, yet the form of the unknown might now in some degree be ascertained. He appeared to be a horseman of large dimensions and mounted on a black horse of powerful frame. He made no offer of molestation or sociability, but kept aloof on one side of the road, jogging along on the blind side of old Gunpowder, who had now got over his fright and waywardness.

Ichabod, who had no relish for this strange midnight companion, and bethought himself of the adventure of Brom Bones with the Galloping Hessian, now quickened his steed in hopes of leaving the companion behind. The stranger, however, quickened his horse to an equal pace. Ichabod pulled up, and fell into a walk, thinking to lag behind; the other did the same. His heart began to sink within him; he endeavored to resume his psalm tune, but his parched tongue clove to the roof of his mouth, and he could not utter a stave. There was something in the moody and dogged silence of this pertinacious companion that was mysterious and appalling. It was soon fearfully accounted for. On mounting a rising ground, which brought the figure of his fellow traveler in relief against the sky, gigantic in height and muffled in a cloak, Ichabod was horror-struck on perceiving that he was headless! But the schoolmaster's horror was still more increased on observing that the head, which should have rested on his shoulders, was carried before him on the pommel of the saddle. Ichabod's terror rose to desperation; he rained a shower of kicks and blows upon Gunpowder, hoping by a sudden movement to give his companion the slip; but the specter started full jump with him. Away, then, they dashed through thick and thin, stones flying and sparks flashing at every bound. Ichabod's flimsy garments fluttered in the air as he stretched his long lank body away over his horse's head in the eagerness of his flight.

They had now reached the road which turns off to Sleepy Hollow; but Gunpowder, who seemed possessed with a demon, instead of keeping up it, made an opposite turn and plunged headlong downhill to the left. This road leads through a sandy hollow shaded by trees for about a quarter of a mile, where it crosses the bridge famous in goblin story, and just beyond swells the green knoll on which stands the whitewashed church.

As yet the panic of the steed had given his unskillful rider an apparent advantage in the chase; but just as he had gotten halfway through the hollow, the girths of the saddle gave away, and he felt it slipping from under him. He seized it by the pommel and endeavored to hold it firm, but in vain, and had just time to save himself by clasping old Gunpowder round the neck, when the saddle fell to the earth, and he heard it trampled underfoot by his pursuer. For a moment the terror of Hans Van Ripper's wrath passed across his mind, for it was his Sunday saddle; but this was no time for petty fears; the goblin was hard on his haunches, and (unskilled rider that he was) he had much ado to maintain his seat, sometimes slipping on one side, sometimes on another, and sometimes jolted on the high ridge of his horse's backbone with a violence that he verily feared would cleave him asunder.

An opening in the trees now cheered him with the hopes that the church bridge was at hand. The wavering reflection of a silver star in the center of the brook told him that he was not mistaken. He saw the walls of the church dimly glaring under the trees beyond. He recollected the place where Brom Bones's ghostly competitor had disappeared. *If I can but reach that bridge,* thought Ichabod, *I am safe.* Just then he heard the black steed panting and blowing close behind him; he even fancied that he felt his hot breath. Another convulsive kick in the ribs, and old Gunpowder sprang upon the bridge; he thundered over the resounding planks; he gained the opposite side; and now Ichabod cast a look behind to see if his pursuer should vanish, according to rule, in a flash of fire and brimstone. Just then he saw the goblin rising in his stirrups, and in the very act of hurling his head at him. Ichabod endeavored to dodge the horrible missile, but too late. It encountered his cranium with a tremendous crash; he was tumbled headlong into the dust, and Gunpowder, the black steed, and the goblin rider passed by like a whirlwind.

The next morning the old horse was found, without his saddle and with the bridle under his feet, soberly cropping the grass at his master's gate. Ichabod did not make his appearance at breakfast; dinner hour came, but no Ichabod. The boys assembled at the schoolhouse and strolled idly about the banks of the brook, but no schoolmaster. Hans Van Ripper now began to feel some uneasiness about the fate of poor Ichabod and his saddle. An inquiry was set on foot, and after diligent investigation they came upon his traces. In one part of the road leading to the church was found the saddle trampled in the dirt; the tracks of horses' hoofs, deeply dented in the road and evidently at furious speed, were traced to the bridge, beyond which, on the bank of a broad part of the brook, where the water ran deep and black, was found the hat of the unfortunate Ichabod, and close beside it a spattered pumpkin.

The brook was searched, but the body of the schoolmaster was not to be discovered. Hans Van Ripper, as executor of Ichabod's estate, examined the bundle which contained all his worldly effects. They consisted of two shirts and a half, two stocks for the neck, a pair or two of worsted stockings, an old pair of corduroy smallclothes, a rusty razor, a book of psalm tunes full of dog's ears, and a broken pitch pipe. As to the books and furniture of the schoolhouse, they belonged to the community, excepting Cotton Mather's history of witchcraft, a New England almanac, and a book of dreams and fortune-telling; in which last was a sheet of foolscap much scribbled and blotted in several fruitless attempts to make a copy of verses in honor of the heiress of Van Tassel. These magic books and the poetic scrawl were forthwith consigned to the flames by Hans Van Ripper, who from that time forward determined to send his children no more to school, observing that he never knew any good come of this same reading and writing. Whatever money the schoolmaster possessed—and he had received his quarter's pay but a day or two before—he must have had about his person at the time of his disappearance.

The mysterious event caused much speculation at the church on the following Sunday. Knots of gazers and gossips were collected in the churchyard, at the bridge, and at the spot where the hat and pumpkin had been found. The stories of Brouwer, of Bones, and a whole budget of others were called to mind, and when they had diligently considered them all, and compared them with the symptoms of the present case, they shook their heads and came to the conclusion that Ichabod had been carried off by the Galloping Hessian. As he was a bachelor and in nobody's debt, nobody troubled his head any more about him, the school was removed to a different quarter of the hollow, and another pedagogue reigned in his stead.

It is true an old farmer, who had been down to New York on a visit several years after, and from whom this account of the ghostly adventure was received, brought home the intelligence that Ichabod Crane was still alive; that he had left the neighborhood, partly through fear of the goblin and Hans Van Ripper, and partly in mortification at having been suddenly dismissed by the heiress; that he had changed his quarters to a distant part of the country, had kept school and studied law at the same time, had been admitted to the bar, turned politician, electioneered, written for the newspapers, and finally had been made a justice of the Ten Pound Court. Brom Bones too, who shortly after his rival's disappearance conducted the blooming Katrina in triumph to the altar, was observed to look exceedingly knowing whenever the story of Ichabod was related, and always burst into a hearty laugh at the mention of the pumpkin; which led some to suspect that he knew more about the matter than he chose to tell.

The old country wives, however, who are the best judges of these matters, maintain to this day that Ichabod was spirited away by supernatural means; and it is a favorite story often told about the neighborhood round the intervening fire. The bridge became more than ever an object of superstitious awe, and that may be the reason why the road has been altered of late years, so as to approach the church by the border of the millpond. The schoolhouse, being deserted, soon fell to decay, and was reported to be haunted by the ghost of the unfortunate pedagogue; and the plowboy, loitering homeward of a still summer evening, has often fancied his voice at a distance chanting a melancholy psalm tune among the tranquil solitudes of Sleepy Hollow.

POSTSCRIPT
Found in the Handwriting of Mr. Knickerbocker

The preceding tale is given almost in the precise words in which I heard it related at a corporation meeting of the ancient city of Manhattoes, at which were present many of its sagest and most illustrious burghers. The narrator was a pleasant, shabby, gentlemanly old fellow in pepper-and-salt clothes, with a sadly humorous face, and one whom I strongly suspected of being poor, he made such efforts to be entertaining. When his story was concluded, there was much laughter and approbation, particularly from two or three deputy aldermen who had been asleep the greater part of the time. There was, however, one tall, dry-looking old gentleman, with beetling eyebrows, who maintained a grave and rather severe face throughout, now and then folding his arms, inclining his head, and looking down upon the floor, as if turning a doubt over in his mind. He was one of your wary men, who never laugh but upon good grounds—when they have reason and the law on their side. When the mirth of the rest of the company had subsided and silence was restored, he leaned one arm on the elbow of his chair, and sticking the other akimbo, demanded, with a slight but exceedingly sage motion of the head and contraction of the brow, what was the moral of the story and what it went to prove.

The storyteller, who was just putting a glass of wine to his lips as a refreshment after his toils, paused for a moment, looked at his inquirer with an air of infinite deference, and, lowering the glass slowly to the table, observed that the story was intended most logically to prove—

"That there is no situation in life but has its advantages and pleasures—provided we will but take a joke as we find it;

"That, therefore, he that runs races with goblin troopers is likely to have rough riding of it.

"Ergo, for a country schoolmaster to be refused the hand of a Dutch heiress is a certain step to high preferment in the state."

The cautious old gentleman knit his brows tenfold closer after this explanation, being sorely puzzled by the ratiocination of the syllogism, while methought the one in pepper-and-salt eyed him with something of a triumphant leer. At length he observed that all this was very well, but still he thought the story a little on the extravagant—there were one or two points on which he had his doubts.

"Faith, sir," replied the storyteller, "as to that matter, I don't believe one half of it myself."

—D.K.

RIP VAN WINKLE

*A Posthumous Writing
of Diedrich Knickerbocker*

*By Woden, God of Saxons,
From whence comes Wensday, that is Wodensday,
Truth is a thing that ever I will keep,
Unto thylke day in which I creep into
My sepulchre—*
—From *The Ordinary*, a comedy by William Cartwright

* * *

Note: The following tale was found among the papers of the late Diedrich Knickerbocker, an old gentleman of New York, who was very curious about the Dutch history of the province and the manners of the descendants from its primitive settlers. His historical researches, however, did not lie so much among books as among men; for the former are lamentably scanty on his favorite topics;

whereas he found the old burghers, and still more, their wives, rich in that legendary lore, so invaluable to true history. Whenever, therefore, he happened upon a genuine Dutch family, snugly shut up in its low-roofed farmhouse, under a spreading sycamore, he looked upon it as a little clasped volume of black letter, and studied it with the zeal of a bookworm.

The result of all these researches was a history of the province, during the reign of the Dutch governors, which he published some years since. There have been various opinions as to the literary character of his work, and, to tell the truth, it is not a whit better than it should be. Its chief merit is its scrupulous accuracy, which indeed was a little questioned on its first appearance, but has since been completely established; and it is now admitted into all historical collections, as a book of unquestionable authority.

The old gentleman died shortly after the publication of his work; and now that he is dead and gone, it cannot do much harm to his memory to say that his time might have been much better employed in weightier labors. He, however, was apt to ride his hobby his own way; and though it did now and then kick up the dust a little in the eyes of his neighbors, and grieve the spirit of some friends, for whom he felt the truest deference and affection, yet his errors and follies are remembered "more in sorrow than in anger," and it begins to be suspected, that he never intended to injure or offend. But however his memory may be appreciated by critics, it is still held dear among many folks, whose good opinion is well worth having; particularly by certain biscuit-bakers, who have gone so far as to imprint his likeness on their New Year cakes, and have thus given him a chance for immortality, almost equal to the being stamped on a Waterloo medal, or a Queen Anne's farthing.

W HOEVER HAS MADE A VOYAGE UP the Hudson must remember the Catskill Mountains. They are a dismembered branch of the great Appalachian family, and are seen away to the west of the river, swelling up to a noble height, and lording it over the surrounding country. Every change of season, every change of weather, indeed, every hour of the day produces some change in the magical hues and shapes of these mountains; and they are regarded by all the good wives, far and near, as perfect barometers. When the weather is fair and settled, they are clothed in blue and purple, and print their bold outlines on the clear evening sky; but sometimes, when the rest of the landscape is cloudless, they will gather a hood of gray vapors about their summits, which, in the last rays of the setting sun, will glow and light up like a crown of glory.

At the foot of these fairy mountains, the voyager may have descried the light smoke curling up from a village, whose shingle roofs gleam among the trees, just where the blue tints of the upland melt away into the fresh green of the nearer landscape. It is a little village of great antiquity, having been founded by some of the Dutch colonists, in the early times of the province, just about the beginning of the government of the good Peter Stuyvesant (may he rest in peace!), and there were some of the houses of the original settlers standing within a few years, built of small yellow bricks, brought from Holland, having latticed windows and gable fronts, surmounted with weathervanes.

In that same village, and in one of these very houses (which, to tell the precise truth, was sadly timeworn and weatherbeaten), there lived, many years since, while the country was yet a province of Great Britain, a simple, good-natured fellow, of the name of Rip Van Winkle. He was a descendant of the Van Winkles who figured so gallantly in the chivalrous days of Peter Stuyvesant, and accompanied him to the siege of Fort Christina. He inherited, however, but little of the martial character of his ancestors. I have observed that he was a simple, good-natured man; he was, moreover, a kind neighbor, and an obedient henpecked husband. Indeed, to the latter circumstance might be owing that meekness of spirit which gained him such universal popularity; for those men are apt to be obsequious and conciliating abroad, who are under the discipline of their wives at home. Their tempers, doubtless, are rendered pliant and malleable in the fiery furnace of domestic tribulation, and a curtain lecture is worth all the sermons in the world for teaching the virtues of patience and long-suffering. A termagant wife may, therefore, in some respects, be considered a tolerable blessing, and if so, Rip Van Winkle was thrice blessed.

Certain it is, that he was a great favorite among all the good wives of the village, who, as usual with the amiable sex, took his part in all family squabbles, and never failed, whenever they talked those matters over in their evening gossipings, to lay all the blame on Dame Van Winkle. The children of the village, too, would shout with joy whenever he approached. He assisted at their sports, made their playthings, taught them to fly kites and shoot marbles, and told them long stories of ghosts and witches. Whenever he went dodging about the village, he was surrounded by a troop of them hanging on his skirts, clambering on his back, and playing a thousand tricks on him with impunity; and not a dog would bark at him throughout the neighborhood.

The great error in Rip's composition was an insuperable aversion to all kinds of profitable labor. It could not be for want of assiduity or perseverance; for he would sit on a wet rock, with a rod as long and heavy as a Tartar's lance, and fish all day without a murmur, even though he should not be encouraged by a single nibble. He would carry a fowling piece on his shoulder, for hours together, trudging through woods and swamps, and uphill and down dale, to shoot a few squirrels or wild pigeons. He would never refuse to assist a neighbor even in the roughest toil, and was a foremost man in all country frolics for husking corn, or building stone fences; the women of the village, too, used to employ him to run their errands, and to do such little odd jobs as their less obliging husbands would not do for them. In a word, Rip was ready to attend to anybody's business but his own; but as to doing family duty, and keeping his farm in order, he found it impossible.

In fact, he declared it was of no use to work on his farm; it was the most pestilent little piece of ground in the whole country; everything about it went wrong, in spite of him. His fences were continually falling to pieces; his cow would either go astray, or get among the cabbages; weeds were sure to grow quicker in his fields than anywhere else; the rain always made a point of setting in just as he had some outdoor work to do; so that though his patrimonial estate had dwindled away under his management, acre by acre, until there was little more left than a mere patch of corn and potatoes, yet it was the worst-conditioned farm in the neighborhood.

His children, too, were as ragged and wild as if they belonged to nobody. His son Rip, an urchin begotten in his own likeness, promised to inherit the habits, with the old clothes, of his father. He was generally seen trooping like a colt at his mother's heels, equipped in a pair of his father's cast-off galligaskins, which he had much ado to hold up with one hand, as a fine lady does her train in bad weather.

Rip Van Winkle, however, was one of those happy mortals, of foolish, well-oiled dispositions, who take the world easy, eat white bread or brown, whichever can be got with least thought or trouble, and would rather starve on a penny than work for a pound. If left to himself, he would have whistled life away, in perfect contentment; but his wife kept continually dinning in his ears about his idleness, his carelessness, and the ruin he was bringing on his family. Morning, noon, and night, her tongue was incessantly going, and everything he said or did was sure to produce a torrent of household eloquence. Rip had but one way of replying to all lectures of the kind, and that, by frequent use, had grown into a habit. He shrugged his shoulders, shook his head, cast up his eyes, but said nothing. This, however, always provoked a fresh volley from his wife, so that he was fain to draw off his forces, and take to the outside of the house—the only side which, in truth, belongs to a henpecked husband.

Rip's sole domestic adherent was his dog, Wolf, who was as much henpecked as his master; for Dame Van Winkle regarded them as companions in idleness, and even looked upon Wolf with an evil eye, as the cause of his master's going so often astray. True it is, in all points of spirit befitting an honorable dog, he was as courageous an animal as ever scoured the woods—but what courage can withstand the evildoing and all-besetting terrors of a woman's tongue? The moment Wolf entered the house, his crest fell, his tail drooped to the ground, or curled between his legs, he sneaked about with a gallows air, casting many a sidelong glance at Dame Van Winkle, and at the least flourish of a broomstick or ladle, he would fly to the door with yelping precipitation.

Times grew worse and worse with Rip Van Winkle as years of matrimony rolled on; a tart temper never mellows with age, and a sharp tongue is the only edged tool that grows keener with constant use. For a long while he used to console himself, when driven from home, by frequenting a kind of perpetual club of the sages, philosophers, and other idle personages of the village, which held its sessions on a bench before a small inn, designated by a rubicund portrait of His Majesty George the Third. Here they used to sit in the shade through a long, lazy summer's day, talking listlessly over village gossip, or telling endless, sleepy stories about nothing. But it would have been worth any statesman's money to have heard the profound discussions which sometimes took place, when by chance an old newspaper fell into their hands from some passing traveler. How solemnly they would listen to the contents, as drawled out by Derrick Van Bummel, the schoolmaster, a dapper learned little man, who was not to be daunted by the most gigantic word in the dictionary; and how sagely they would deliberate upon public events some months after they had taken place.

The opinions of this junto were completely controlled by Nicholas Vedder, a patriarch of the village, and landlord of the inn, at the door of which he took his seat from morning till night, just moving sufficiently to avoid the sun, and keep in the shade of a large tree; so that the neighbors could tell the hour by his movements as accurately as by a sundial. It is true, he was rarely heard to speak, but smoked his pipe incessantly. His adherents, however (for every great man has his adherents), perfectly understood him, and knew how to gather his opinions. When anything that was read or related displeased him, he was observed to smoke his pipe vehemently, and to send forth short, frequent, and angry puffs; but when pleased, he would inhale the smoke slowly and tranquilly, and emit it in light and placid clouds, and sometimes, taking the pipe from his mouth, and letting the fragrant vapor curl about his nose, would gravely nod his head in token of perfect approbation.

From even this stronghold the unlucky Rip was at length routed by his termagant wife, who would suddenly break in upon the tranquility of the assemblage, and call the members all to naught; nor was that august personage, Nicholas Vedder himself, sacred from the daring tongue of this terrible virago, who charged him outright with encouraging her husband in habits of idleness.

Poor Rip was at last reduced almost to despair; and his

only alternative, to escape from the labor of the farm and the clamor of his wife, was to take gun in hand, and stroll away into the woods. Here he would sometimes seat himself at the foot of a tree, and share the contents of his wallet with Wolf, with whom he sympathized as a fellow sufferer in persecution. "Poor Wolf," he would say, "thy mistress leads thee a dog's life of it, but never mind, my lad; whilst I live, thou shalt never want a friend to stand by thee!" Wolf would wag his tail, look wistfully into his master's face, and if dogs can feel pity, I verily believe he reciprocated the sentiment with all his heart.

In a long ramble of the kind, on a fine autumnal day, Rip had unconsciously scrambled to one of the highest parts of the Catskill Mountains. He was after his favorite sport of squirrel-shooting, and the still solitudes had echoed and re-echoed with the reports of his gun. Panting and fatigued, he threw himself, late in the afternoon, onto a green knoll, covered with mountain herbage, that crowned the brow of a precipice. From an opening between the trees, he could overlook all the lower country for many a mile of rich woodland. He saw at a distance the lordly Hudson, far, far below him, moving on its silent but majestic course, with the reflection of a purple cloud, or the sail of a lagging bark, here and there sleeping on its glassy body and at last losing itself in the blue highlands.

On the other side he looked down into a deep mountain glen, wild, lonely, and shagged, the bottom filled with fragments from the impending cliffs, and scarcely lighted by the reflected rays of the setting sun. For some time Rip lay musing on this scene; evening was gradually advancing; the mountains began to throw their long blue shadows over the valleys; he saw that it would be dark long before he could reach the village; and he heaved a heavy sigh when he thought of encountering the terrors of Dame Van Winkle.

As he was about to descend, he heard a voice from a distance hallooing, "Rip Van Winkle! Rip Van Winkle!" He looked around, but could see nothing but a crow winging its solitary flight across the mountain. He thought his fancy must have deceived him, and turned again to descend, when he heard the same cry ring through the still evening air, "Rip Van Winkle! Rip Van Winkle!" At the same time Wolf bristled up his back, and giving a low growl, skulked to his master's side, looking fearfully down into the glen. Rip now felt a vague apprehension stealing over him; he looked anxiously in the same direction, and perceived a strange figure slowly toiling up the rocks, and bending under the weight of something he carried on his back. He was surprised to see any human being in this lonely and unfrequented place, but supposing it to be someone of the neighborhood in need of his assistance, he hastened down to yield it.

On nearer approach, he was still more surprised at the singularity of the stranger's appearance. He was a short, square-built old fellow, with thick bushy hair, and a grizzled beard.

His dress was of the antique Dutch fashion—a cloth jerkin strapped round the waist—several pairs of breeches, the outer one of ample volume, decorated with rows of buttons down the sides, and bunches at the knees. He bore on his shoulders a stout keg, that seemed full of liquor, and made signs for Rip to approach and assist him with the load. Though rather shy and distrustful of this new acquaintance, Rip complied with his usual alacrity; and mutually relieving each other, they clambered up a narrow gully, apparently the dry bed of a mountain torrent. As they ascended, Rip every now and then heard long rolling peals, like distant thunder, that seemed to issue out of a deep ravine, or rather cleft between lofty rocks, toward which their rugged path conducted. He paused for an instant, but supposing it to be the muttering of one of those transient thundershowers which often take place in the mountain heights, he proceeded. Passing through the ravine, they came to a hollow, like a small amphitheater, surrounded by perpendicular precipices, over the brinks of which impending trees shot their branches, so that you only caught glimpses of the azure sky, and the bright evening cloud. During the whole time Rip and his companion had labored on in silence; for though the former marveled greatly what could be the object of carrying a keg of liquor up this wild mountain, yet there was something strange and incomprehensible about the unknown, that inspired awe, and checked familiarity.

On entering the amphitheater, new objects of wonder

presented themselves. On a level spot in the center was a company of odd-looking personages playing at ninepins. They were dressed in quaint outlandish fashion; some wore short doublets, others jerkins, with long knives in their belts, and most of them had enormous breeches, of similar style with that of the guide's. Their visages, too, were peculiar; one had a large head, broad face, and small piggish eyes; the face of another seemed to consist entirely of nose, and was surmounted by a white sugarloaf hat, set off with a little red rooster's tail. They all had beards, of various shapes and colors. There was one who seemed to be the commander. He was a stout old gentleman, with a weather-beaten countenance; he wore a laced doublet, broad belt and hanger, high-crowned hat and feather, red stockings, and high-heeled shoes, with roses in them. The whole group reminded Rip of the figures in an old Flemish painting, in the parlor of Dominie Van Schaick, the village parson, and which had been brought over from Holland at the time of the settlement.

What seemed particularly odd to Rip was, that though these folks were evidently amusing themselves, yet they maintained the gravest faces, the most mysterious silence, and were, withal, the most melancholy party of pleasure he had ever witnessed. Nothing interrupted the stillness of the scene but the noise of the balls, which, whenever they were rolled, echoed along the mountains like rumbling peals of thunder.

As Rip and his companion approached them, they suddenly

desisted from their play, and stared at him with such a fixed statue-like gaze, and such strange uncouth, lackluster countenances, that his heart turned within him, and his knees smote together. His companion now emptied the contents of the keg into large flagons, and made signs to him to wait upon the company. He obeyed with fear and trembling; they quaffed the liquor in profound silence, and then returned to their game.

By degrees, Rip's awe and apprehension subsided. He even ventured, when no eye was fixed upon him, to taste the beverage, which he found had much of the flavor of excellent Hollands. He was naturally a thirsty soul, and was soon tempted to repeat the draft. One taste provoked another; and he reiterated his visits to the flagon so often, that at length his senses were overpowered, his eyes swam in his head, his head gradually declined, and he fell into a deep sleep.

On waking, he found himself on the green knoll whence he had first seen the old man of the glen. He rubbed his eyes—it was a bright sunny morning. The birds were hopping and twittering among the bushes, and the eagle was wheeling aloft, and breasting the pure mountain breeze. *Surely,* thought Rip, *I have not slept here all night.* He recalled the occurrences before he fell asleep. The strange man with the keg of liquor—the mountain ravine—the wild retreat among the rocks—the woebegone party at ninepins—the flagon—*Oh! That flagon! That wicked flagon!* thought Rip. *What excuse shall I make to Dame Van Winkle?*

He looked round for his gun, but in place of the clean well-oiled fowling piece, he found an old firelock lying by him, the barrel encrusted with rust, the lock falling off, and the stock worm-eaten. He now suspected that the grave roysterers of the mountains had put a trick upon him, and, having dosed him with liquor, had robbed him of his gun. Wolf, too, had disappeared, but he might have strayed away after a squirrel or partridge. He whistled after him and shouted his name, but all in vain; the echoes repeated his whistle and shout, but no dog was to be seen.

He determined to revisit the scene of the last evening's gambol, and if he met with any of the party, to demand his dog and gun. As he rose to walk, he found himself stiff in the joints, and wanting in his usual activity. *These mountain beds do not agree with me,* thought Rip, *and if this frolic should lay me up with a fit of the rheumatism, I shall have a blessed time with Dame Van Winkle.* With some difficulty he got down into the glen; he found the gully up which he and his companion had ascended the preceding evening, but to his astonishment a mountain stream was now foaming down it, leaping from rock to rock, and filling the glen with babbling murmurs. He, however, made shift to scramble up its sides, working his toilsome way through thickets of birch, sassafras, and witch hazel; and sometimes tripped up or entangled by the wild grapevines that twisted their coils and tendrils from tree to tree, and spread a kind of network in his path.

At length he reached where the ravine had opened through the cliffs to the amphitheater; but no traces of such opening remained. The rocks presented a high impenetrable wall, over which the torrent came tumbling in a sheet of feathery foam, and fell into a broad deep basin, black from the shadows of the surrounding forest. Here, then, poor Rip was brought to a stand. He again called and whistled after his dog; he was only answered by the cawing of a flock of idle crows, sporting high in the air about a dry tree that overhung a sunny precipice; and who, secure in their elevation, seemed to look down and scoff at the poor man's perplexities. What was to be done? The morning was passing away, and Rip felt famished for want of his breakfast. He grieved to give up his dog and gun; he dreaded to meet his wife; but it would not do to starve among the mountains. He shook his head, shouldered the rusty firelock, and, with a heart full of trouble and anxiety, turned his steps homeward.

As he approached the village, he met a number of people, but none whom he knew, which somewhat surprised him, for he had thought himself acquainted with everyone in the country round. Their dress, too, was of a different fashion from that to which he was accustomed. They all stared at him with equal marks of surprise, and whenever they cast eyes upon him, invariably stroked their chins. The constant recurrence of this gesture induced Rip, involuntarily, to do the same—when, to his astonishment, he found his beard had grown a foot long!

He had now entered the skirts of the village. A troop of strange children ran at his heels, hooting after him, and pointing at his gray beard. The dogs, too, not one of which he recognized for an old acquaintance, barked at him as he passed. The very village was altered: it was larger and more populous. There were rows of houses which he had never seen before, and those which had been his familiar haunts had disappeared. Strange names were over the doors—strange faces at the windows—everything was strange. His mind now misgave him; he began to doubt whether both he and the world around him were not bewitched. Surely this was his native village, which he had left but a day before. There stood the Catskill Mountains—there ran the silver Hudson at a distance—there was every hill and dale precisely as it had always been—Rip was sorely perplexed— *That flagon last night*, thought he, *has addled my poor head sadly!*

It was with some difficulty that he found the way to his own house, which he approached with silent awe, expecting every moment to hear the shrill voice of Dame Van Winkle. He found the house gone to decay—the roof had fallen in, the windows shattered, and the doors off the hinges. A half-starved dog that looked like Wolf was skulking about it. Rip called him by name, but the cur snarled, showed his teeth, and passed on. This was an unkind cut indeed.

"My very dog," sighed poor Rip, "has forgotten me!"

He entered the house, which, to tell the truth, Dame Van

Winkle had always kept in neat order. It was empty, forlorn, and apparently abandoned. This desolateness overcame all his connubial fears; he called loudly for his wife and children; the lonely chambers rang for a moment with his voice, and then all again was silence.

He now hurried forth, and hastened to his old resort, the village inn—but it too was gone. A large rickety wooden building stood in its place, with great gaping windows, some of them broken, and mended with old hats and petticoats, and over the door was painted THE UNION HOTEL, BY JONATHAN DOOLITTLE. Instead of the great tree that used to shelter the quiet little Dutch inn of yore, there now was reared a tall naked pole, with something on the top that looked like a red nightcap, and from it was fluttering a flag, on which was a singular assemblage of stars and stripes—all this was strange and incomprehensible. He recognized on the sign, however, the ruby face of King George, under which he had smoked so many a peaceful pipe, but even this was singularly metamorphosed. The red coat was changed for one of blue and buff, a sword was held in the hand instead of a scepter, the head was decorated with a tricorner hat, and underneath was painted in large characters, GENERAL WASHINGTON.

There was, as usual, a crowd of folk about the door, but none that Rip recollected. The very character of the people seemed changed. There was a busy, bustling, disputatious tone about it, instead of the accustomed phlegm and drowsy tranquility. He looked in vain for the sage Nicholas Vedder, with his broad face, double chin, and fair long pipe, uttering clouds of tobacco smoke, instead of idle speeches; or Van Bummel, the schoolmaster, doling forth the contents of an ancient newspaper. In place of these, a lean, bilious-looking fellow, with his pockets full of handbills, was haranguing, vehemently about rights of citizens-elections—members of Congress—liberty—Bunker Hill—heroes of seventy-six, and other words, which were a perfect Babylonish jargon to the bewildered Van Winkle.

The appearance of Rip, with his long, grizzled beard, his rusty fowling piece, his uncouth dress, and the army of women and children at his heels, soon attracted the attention of the tavern politicians. They crowded round him, eying him from head to foot, with great curiosity. The orator bustled up to him, and, drawing him partly aside, inquired, "on which side he voted?" Rip stared in vacant stupidity. Another short but busy little fellow pulled him by the arm, and rising on tiptoe, inquired in his ear, "whether he was Federal or Democrat." Rip was equally at a loss to comprehend the question; when a knowing, self-important old gentleman, in a sharp tricorner hat, made his way through the crowd, putting them to the right and left with his elbows as he passed, and planting himself before Van Winkle, with one arm akimbo, the other resting on his cane, his keen eyes and sharp hat penetrating, as it were, into his very soul, demanded in an austere tone, "What brought him to the election with a gun on his shoulder, and a mob at his heels; and whether he meant to breed a riot in the village?"

"Alas! Gentlemen," cried Rip, somewhat dismayed, "I am a poor, quiet man, a native of the place, and a loyal subject of the king, God bless him!"

Here a general shout burst from the bystanders—"A tory! A tory! A spy! A refugee! Hustle him! Away with him!" It was with great difficulty that the self-important man in the tricorner hat restored order; and having assumed a tenfold austerity of brow, demanded again of the unknown culprit what he came there for, and whom he was seeking. The poor man humbly assured him that he meant no harm, but merely came there in search of some of his neighbors, who used to keep about the tavern.

"Well, who are they? Name them."

Rip bethought himself a moment, and inquired, "Where's Nicholas Vedder?"

There was a silence for a little while, when an old man replied, in a thin, piping voice, "Nicholas Vedder? Why, he is dead and gone these eighteen years! There was a wooden tombstone in the churchyard that used to tell all about him, but that's rotten and gone too."

"Where's Brom Dutcher?"

"Oh, he went off to the army in the beginning of the war;

some say he was killed at the storming of Stony Point; others say he was drowned in a squall at the foot of Anthony's Nose. I don't know; he never came back again."

"Where's Van Bummel, the schoolmaster?"

"He went off to the war, too; was a great militia general, and is now in Congress."

Rip's heart died away, at hearing of these sad changes in his home and friends, and finding himself thus alone in the world. Every answer puzzled him too, by treating of such enormous lapses of time, and of matters which he could not understand: war—Congress—Stony Point. He had no courage to ask after any more friends, but cried out in despair, "Does nobody here know Rip Van Winkle?"

"Oh, Rip Van Winkle!" exclaimed two or three. "Oh, to be sure! That's Rip Van Winkle yonder, leaning against the tree."

Rip looked, and beheld a precise counterpart of himself as he went up the mountain; apparently as lazy, and certainly as ragged. The poor fellow was now completely confounded. He doubted his own identity, and whether he was himself or another man. In the midst of his bewilderment, the man in the tricorner hat demanded who he was, and what was his name?

"God knows!" exclaimed he at his wit's end. "I'm not myself—I'm somebody else—that's me yonder—no—that's somebody else, got into my shoes—I was myself last night, but I fell asleep on the mountain, and they've changed my gun, and everything's changed, and I'm changed, and I can't tell what's my name, or who I am!"

The bystanders began now to look at each other, nod, wink significantly, and tap their fingers against their foreheads. There was a whisper, also, about securing the gun, and keeping the old fellow from doing mischief; at the very suggestion of which, the self-important man with the tricorner hat retired with some precipitation. At this critical moment a fresh, comely woman pressed through the throng to get a peep at the gray-bearded man. She had a chubby child in her arms, which, frightened at his looks, began to cry. "Hush, Rip," cried she, "hush, you little fool; the old man won't hurt you." The name of the child, the air of the mother, the tone of her voice, all awakened a train of recollections in his mind.

"What is your name, my good woman?" asked he.

"Judith Cardenier."

"And your father's name?"

"Ah, poor man, Rip Van Winkle was his name, but it's twenty years since he went away from home with his gun, and never has been heard of since. His dog came home without him; but whether he shot himself, or was carried away by others, nobody can tell. I was then but a little girl."

Rip had but one more question to ask; but he put it with a faltering voice:

"Where's your mother?"

Oh, she too had died but a short time since; she broke a blood vessel in a fit of passion at a New England peddler.

There was a drop of comfort, at least, in this intelligence. The honest man could contain himself no longer. He caught his daughter and her child in his arms. "I am your father!" cried he. "Young Rip Van Winkle once—old Rip Van Winkle now. Does nobody know poor Rip Van Winkle!"

All stood amazed, until an old woman, tottering out from among the crowd, put her hand to her brow, and peering under it into his face for a moment exclaimed, "Sure enough! It is Rip Van Winkle—it is himself. Welcome home again, old neighbor. Why, where have you been these twenty long years?"

Rip's story was soon told, for the whole twenty years had been to him but as one night. The neighbors stared when they heard it; some were seen to wink at each other, and put their tongues in their cheeks; and the self-important man in the tricorner hat, who, when the alarm was over, had returned to the field, screwed down the corners of his mouth, and shook his head—upon which there was a general shaking of the head throughout the assemblage.

It was determined, however, to take the opinion of old Peter Vanderdonk, who was seen slowly advancing up the road. He was a descendant of the historian of that name, who wrote one of the earliest accounts of the province. Peter was the most ancient inhabitant of the village, and well versed in all the wonderful events and traditions of the neighborhood.

He recollected Rip at once, and corroborated his story in the most satisfactory manner. He assured the company that it was a fact, handed down from his ancestor, the historian, that the Catskill Mountains had always been haunted by strange beings. That it was affirmed that the great Henry Hudson, the first European visitor of the river and country, kept a kind of vigil there every twenty years, with his crew of the *Half Moon*; being permitted in this way to revisit the scenes of his enterprise, and keep a guardian eye upon the river and the great city called by his name. That Peter's father had once seen them in their old Dutch dresses playing at ninepins in the hollow of the mountain; and that he himself had heard, one summer afternoon, the sound of their balls, like distant peals of thunder.

To make a long story short, the company broke up, and returned to the more important concerns of the election. Rip's daughter took him home to live with her; she had a snug, well-furnished house, and a stout cheery farmer for a husband, whom Rip recollected for one of the urchins that used to climb upon his back. As to Rip's son and heir, who was the ditto of himself, seen leaning against the tree, he was employed to work on the farm; but evinced a hereditary disposition to attend to anything else but his business.

Rip now resumed his old walks and habits; he soon found many of his former cronies, though all rather the worse for the wear and tear of time; and preferred making friends among the rising generation, with whom he soon grew into great favor.

Having nothing to do at home, and being arrived at that happy age when a man can be idle with impunity, he took his place once more on the bench, at the inn door, and was reverenced as one of the patriarchs of the village, and a chronicle of the old times "before the war." It was some time before he could get into the regular track of gossip, or could be made to comprehend the strange events that had taken place during his torpor. How that there had been a revolutionary war—that the country had thrown off the yoke of old England—and that, instead of being a subject to His Majesty George the Third, he was now a free citizen of the United States. Rip, in fact, was no politician; the changes of states and empires made but little impression on him; but there was one species of despotism under which he had long groaned, and that was—petticoat government. Happily, that was at an end; he had gotten his neck out of the yoke of matrimony, and could go in and out whenever he pleased, without dreading the tyranny of Dame Van Winkle. Whenever her name was mentioned, however, he shook his head, shrugged his shoulders, and cast up his eyes; which might pass either for an expression of resignation to his fate, or joy at his deliverance.

He used to tell his story to every stranger that arrived at Mr. Doolittle's hotel. He was observed, at first, to vary on some points every time he told it, which was, doubtless, owing to his having so recently awaked. It at last settled down precisely to the tale I have related, and not a man, woman, or child in the neighborhood but knew it by heart. Some always pretended to doubt the reality of it, and insisted that Rip had been out of his head, and that this was one point on which he always remained flighty. The old Dutch inhabitants, however, almost universally gave it full credit. Even to this day, they never hear a thunderstorm of a summer afternoon about the Catskills, but they say Henry Hudson and his crew are at their game of ninepins; and it is a common wish of all henpecked husbands in the neighborhood, when life hangs heavy on their hands, that they might have a quieting draft out of Rip Van Winkle's flagon.

NOTE

The foregoing tale, one would suspect, had been suggested to Mr. Knickerbocker by a little German superstition about the Emperor Frederick der Rothbart and the Kyffhäuser Mountains; the subjoined note, however, which had appended to the tale, shows that it is an absolute fact, narrated with his usual fidelity.

> The story of Rip Van Winkle may seem incredible to many, but nevertheless I give it my full belief, for I know the vicinity of our old Dutch settlements to have been very subject to marvelous events and appearances.

Indeed, I have heard many stranger stories than this, in the villages along the Hudson; all of which were too well authenticated to admit of a doubt. I have even talked with Rip Van Winkle myself, who, when last I saw him, was a very venerable old man, and so perfectly rational and consistent on every other point, that I think no conscientious person could refuse to take this into the bargain; nay, I have seen a certificate on the subject taken before a country justice, and signed with cross, in the justice's own handwriting. The story, therefore, is beyond the possibility of doubt.

—D.K.

POSTSCRIPT

The following are traveling notes from a memorandum book of Mr. Knickerbocker:

> The Kaatsberg or Catskill Mountains have always been a region full of fable. The Native Americans considered them the abode of spirits, who influenced the weather, spreading sunshine or clouds over the landscape, and sending good or bad hunting seasons. They were ruled by an old squaw spirit, said to be their mother. She dwelled on the highest peak of the Catskills, and had charge of the doors of day and night to open and

shut them at the proper hour. She hung up the new moons in the skies, and cut up the old ones into stars. In times of drought, if properly propitiated, she would spin light summer clouds out of cobwebs and morning dew, and send them off from the crest of the mountain, flake after flake, like flakes of carded cotton, to float in the air; until, dissolved by the heat of the sun, they would fall in gentle showers, causing the grass to spring, the fruits to ripen, and the corn to grow an inch an hour. If displeased, however, she would brew up clouds as black as ink, sitting in the midst of them like a bottle-bellied spider in the midst of its web; and when these clouds broke, woe betide the valleys!

In old times, say the Native American traditions, there was a kind of manitou or spirit, who kept about the wildest recesses of the Catskill Mountains, and took a mischievous pleasure in wreaking all kind of evils and vexations upon the Native Americans. Sometimes he would assume the form of a bear, a panther, or a deer, lead the bewildered hunter a weary chase through tangled forests and among ragged rocks, and then spring off with a loud "Ho! Ho!" leaving him aghast on the brink of a beetling precipice or raging torrent.

The favorite abode of this manitou is still shown. It is a rock or cliff on the loneliest port of the mountains, and, from the flowering vines which clamber about it, and the wild flowers which abound in its neighborhood, is known by the name of the Garden Rock. Near the foot of it is a small lake, the haunt of the solitary bittern, with water snakes basking in the sun on the leaves of the pond lilies which lie on the surface. This place was held in great awe by the Native Americans, insomuch that the boldest hunter would not pursue his game within its precincts. Once upon a time, however, a hunter who had lost his way penetrated to the Garden Rock, where he beheld a number of gourds placed in the crotches of trees. One of these he seized and made off with, but in the hurry of his retreat he let it fall among the rocks, when a great stream gushed forth, which washed him away and swept him down precipices, where he was dashed to pieces, and the stream made its way to the Hudson, and continues to flow to the present day, being the identical stream known by the name of the Kaaterskill.

THE INN KITCHEN

"Shall I not take mine ease in mine inn?"
—Falstaff in Shakespeare's Henry IV, Part 1

DURING A JOURNEY THAT I ONCE MADE through the Netherlands, I had arrived one evening at the Pomme d'Or, the principal inn of a small Flemish village. It was after the hour of the table d'hôte, so that I was obliged to make a solitary supper from the relics of its ampler board. The weather was chilly; I was seated alone in one end of a great gloomy dining room, and, my repast being over, I had the prospect before me of a long dull evening, without any visible means of enlivening it. I summoned mine host and requested something to read; he brought me the whole literary stock of his household, a Dutch family Bible, an almanac in the same language, and a number of old Paris newspapers. As I sat dozing over one of the latter, reading old news and stale criticisms, my ear was now and then struck with bursts of laughter which seemed to proceed from the kitchen. Everyone that has traveled on the Continent must know how favorite a resort the kitchen of a country inn is to the middle and inferior order of travelers, particularly in that equivocal kind of weather when a fire becomes agreeable toward evening. I threw aside the newspaper and explored my way to the kitchen, to take a peep at the group that appeared to be so merry. It was composed partly of travelers who had arrived some hours before in a stagecoach, and partly of the usual attendants and hangers-on of inns. They were seated round a great burnished stove, that might have been mistaken for an altar at which they were worshipping. It was covered with various kitchen vessels of resplendent brightness, among which steamed and hissed a huge copper teakettle. A large lamp threw a strong mass of light upon the group, bringing out many odd features in strong relief. Its yellow rays partially illumined the spacious kitchen, dying duskily away into remote corners, except where they settled in mellow radiance on the broad side of a flitch of bacon or were reflected back from well-scoured utensils that gleamed from the midst of obscurity. A strapping Flemish lass, with long golden pendants in her ears and a necklace with a golden heart suspended to it, was the presiding priestess of the temple.

Many of the company were furnished with pipes, and most of them with some kind of evening potation. I found their mirth was occasioned by anecdotes which a little swarthy Frenchman, with a dry wizened face and large whiskers, was giving of his love adventures; at the end of each of which there was one of those bursts of honest unceremonious laughter in which a man indulges in that temple of true liberty, an inn.

As I had no better mode of getting through a tedious blustering evening, I took my seat near the stove, and listened to a variety of travelers' tales, some very extravagant and most very dull. All of them, however, have faded from my treacherous memory except one, which I will endeavor to relate. I fear, however, it derived its chief zest from the manner in which it was told, and the peculiar air and appearance of the narrator. He was a corpulent old Swiss, who had the look of a veteran traveler. He was dressed in a tarnished green traveling jacket, with a broad belt round his waist, and a pair of overalls with buttons from the hips to the ankles. He was of a full rubicund countenance, with a double chin, aquiline nose, and a pleasant twinkling eye. His hair was light, and curled from under an old green velvet traveling cap stuck onto one side of his head. He was interrupted more than once by the arrival of guests or the remarks of his auditors, and paused now and then to replenish his pipe; at which times he had generally a roguish leer and a sly joke for the buxom kitchen maid.

I wish my readers could imagine the old fellow lolling in a huge armchair, one arm akimbo, the other holding a curiously twisted tobacco pipe formed of genuine meerschaum, decorated with silver chain and silken tassel, his head tilted on one side, and a whimsical cut of the eye occasionally as he related the following story.

THE SPECTER BRIDEGROOM

A Traveler's Tale[2]

> He that supper for is dight,
> He lyes full cold, I trow, this night!
> Yestreen to chamber I him led,
> This night Gray-steel has made his bed!
> —From *The History of Sir Eger, Sir Grahame, and Sir Gray-Steel*

ON THE SUMMIT OF ONE OF THE HEIGHTS of the Odenwald, a wild and romantic tract of upper Germany that lies not far from the confluence of the Main and the Rhine, there stood many, many years since the castle of the Baron Von Landshort. It is now quite fallen to decay, and almost buried among beech trees and dark firs; above which, however, its old watchtower may still be seen

---

[2]. The erudite reader, well versed in good-for-nothing lore, will perceive that the above tale must have been suggested to the old Swiss by a little French anecdote, a circumstance said to have taken place in Paris.

struggling, like the former possessor I have mentioned, to carry a high head and look down upon the neighboring country.

The baron was a dry branch of the great family of Katzenellenbogen,[3] and inherited the relics of the property and all the pride of his ancestors. Though the warlike disposition of his predecessors had much impaired the family possessions, yet the baron still endeavored to keep up some show of former state. The times were peaceable, and the German nobles in general had abandoned their inconvenient old castles, perched like eagles' nests among the mountains, and had built more convenient residences in the valleys; still, the baron remained proudly drawn up in his little fortress, cherishing with hereditary inveteracy all the old family feuds, so that he was on ill terms with some of his nearest neighbors, on account of disputes that had happened between their great-great-grandfathers.

The baron had but one child, a daughter, but nature, when she grants but one child, always compensates by making it a prodigy; and so it was with the daughter of the baron. All the nurses, gossips, and country cousins assured her father that she had not her equal for beauty in all Germany; and who should know better than they? She had, moreover, been

---

3. That is, "cat's elbow"—the name of a family of those parts, and very powerful in former times. The appellation, we are told, was given in compliment to a peerless dame of the family, celebrated for a fine arm.

brought up with great care under the superintendence of two maiden aunts, who had spent some years of their early life at one of the little German courts, and were skilled in all branches of knowledge necessary to the education of a fine lady. Under their instructions she became a miracle of accomplishments. By the time she was eighteen, she could embroider to admiration, and had worked whole histories of the saints into tapestry with such strength of expression in their countenances that they looked like so many souls in purgatory. She could read without great difficulty, and had spelled her way through several church legends and almost all the chivalric wonders of the *Heldenbuch*. She had even made considerable proficiency in writing; could sign her own name without missing a letter, and so legibly that her aunts could read it without spectacles. She excelled in making little elegant good-for-nothing, ladylike knickknacks of all kinds, was versed in the most abstruse dancing of the day, played a number of airs on the harp and guitar, and knew all the tender ballads of the Minnelieders by heart.

Her aunts, too, having been great flirts and coquettes in their younger days, were admirably calculated to be vigilant guardians and strict censors of the conduct of their niece; for there is no duenna so rigidly prudent and inexorably decorous as a superannuated coquette. She was rarely suffered out of their sight; never went beyond the domains of the castle unless well attended, or rather well watched; had continual lectures read to her about strict decorum and implicit obedience; and, as to the men—pah!—she was taught to hold them at such a distance and in such absolute distrust that, unless properly authorized, she would not have cast a glance upon the handsomest cavalier in the world—no, not if he were even dying at her feet.

The good effects of this system were wonderfully apparent. The young lady was a pattern of docility and correctness. While others were wasting their sweetness in the glare of the world, and liable to be plucked and thrown aside by every hand, she was coyly blooming into fresh and lovely womanhood under the protection of those immaculate spinsters, like a rosebud blushing forth among guardian thorns. Her aunts looked upon her with pride and exultation, and vaunted that, though all the other young ladies in the world might go astray, yet thank heaven, nothing of the kind could happen to the heiress of Katzenellenbogen.

But, however scantily the Baron Von Landshort might be provided with children, his household was by no means a small one; for providence had enriched him with abundance of poor relations. They, one and all, possessed the affectionate disposition common to humble relatives—were wonderfully attached to the baron, and took every possible occasion to come in swarms and enliven the castle. All family festivals were commemorated by these good people at the baron's expense; and when they were filled with good cheer, they would declare that there was nothing on earth so delightful as these family meetings, these jubilees of the heart.

The baron, though a small man, had a large soul, and it swelled with satisfaction at the consciousness of being the greatest man in the little world about him. He loved to tell long stories about the stark old warriors whose portraits looked grimly down from the walls around, and he found no listeners equal to those who fed at his expense. He was much given to the marvelous and a firm believer in all those supernatural tales with which every mountain and valley in Germany abounds. The faith of his guests exceeded even his own; they listened to every tale of wonder with open eyes and mouth, and never failed to be astonished, even though repeated for the hundredth time. Thus lived the Baron Von Landshort, the oracle of his table, the absolute monarch of his little territory, and happy, above all things, in the persuasion that he was the wisest man of the age.

At the time of which my story treats there was a great family gathering at the castle on an affair of the utmost importance: it was to receive the destined bridegroom of the baron's daughter. A negotiation had been carried on between the father and an old nobleman of Bavaria to unite the dignity of their houses by the marriage of their children. The preliminaries had been conducted with proper punctilio. The young people were betrothed without seeing each other, and the time was appointed for the marriage ceremony. The young Count

Von Altenburg had been recalled from the army for the purpose, and was actually on his way to the baron's to receive his bride. Missives had even been received from him from Würzburg, where he was accidentally detained, mentioning the day and hour when he might be expected to arrive.

The castle was in a tumult of preparation to give him a suitable welcome. The fair bride had been decked out with uncommon care. The two aunts had superintended her toilet, and quarreled the whole morning about every article of her dress. The young lady had taken advantage of their contest to follow the bent of her own taste; and fortunately it was a good one. She looked as lovely as a youthful bridegroom could desire, and the flutter of expectation heightened the luster of her charms.

The suffusions that mantled her face and neck, the gentle heaving of the chest, the eye now and then lost in reverie, all betrayed the soft tumult that was going on in her little heart. The aunts were continually hovering around her, for maiden aunts are apt to take great interest in affairs of this nature. They were giving her a world of staid counsel about how to deport herself, what to say, and in what manner to receive the expected lover.

The baron was no less busied in preparations. He had, in truth, nothing exactly to do; but he was naturally a fuming, bustling little man, and could not remain passive when all the world was in a hurry. He worried from top to bottom of the castle with an air of infinite anxiety; he continually called the servants from their work to exhort them to be diligent; and buzzed about every hall and chamber, as idly restless and importunate as a bluebottle fly on a warm summer's day.

In the meantime the fatted calf had been killed; the forests had rung with the clamor of the huntsmen; the kitchen was crowded with good cheer; the cellars had yielded up whole oceans of Rhein-wein and Ferre-wein; and even the great Heidelberg tun had been laid under contribution. Everything was ready to receive the distinguished guest with Saus und Braus in the true spirit of German hospitality; but the guest delayed to make his appearance. Hour rolled after hour. The sun, that had poured his downward rays upon the rich forest of the Odenwald, now just gleamed along the summits of the mountains. The baron mounted the highest tower and strained his eyes in hopes of catching a distant sight of the count and his attendants. Once he thought he beheld them; the sound of horns came floating from the valley, prolonged by the mountain echoes. A number of horsemen were seen far below, slowly advancing along the road; but when they had nearly reached the foot of the mountain, they suddenly struck off in a different direction. The last ray of sunshine departed, the bats began to flit by in the twilight, the road grew dimmer and dimmer to the view, and nothing appeared stirring in it but now and then a peasant lagging homeward from his labor.

While the old castle of Landshort was in this state of perplexity, a very interesting scene was transacting in a different part of the Odenwald.

The young Count Von Altenburg was tranquilly pursuing his route in that sober jog-trot way in which a man travels toward matrimony when his friends have taken all the trouble and uncertainty of courtship off his hands and a bride is waiting for him as certainly as a dinner at the end of his journey. He had encountered at Würzburg a youthful companion-in-arms with whom he had seen some service on the frontiers—Herman Von Starkenfaust, one of the stoutest hands and worthiest hearts of German chivalry—who was now returning from the army. His father's castle was not far distant from the old fortress of Landshort, although a hereditary feud rendered the families hostile and strangers to each other.

In the warmhearted moment of recognition the young friends related all their past adventures and fortunes, and the count gave the whole history of his intended nuptials with a young lady whom he had never seen, but of whose charms he had received the most enrapturing descriptions.

As the route of the friends lay in the same direction, they agreed to perform the rest of their journey together, and that they might do it the more leisurely, set off from Würzburg at an early hour, the count having given directions for his retinue to follow and overtake him.

They beguiled their wayfaring with recollections of their military scenes and adventures; but the count was apt to be a little tedious now and then about the reputed charms of his bride and the felicity that awaited him.

In this way they had entered among the mountains of the Odenwald, and were traversing one of its most lonely and thickly wooded passes. It is well known that the forests of Germany have always been as much infested by robbers as its castles by specters; and at this time the former were particularly numerous, from the hordes of disbanded soldiers wandering about the country. It will not appear extraordinary, therefore, that the cavaliers were attacked by a gang of these stragglers, in the midst of the forest. They defended themselves with bravery, but were nearly overpowered, when the count's retinue arrived to their assistance. At sight of them the robbers fled, but not until the count had received a mortal wound. He was slowly and carefully conveyed back to the city of Würzburg, and a friar summoned from a neighboring convent who was famous for his skill in administering to both soul and body; but half of his skill was superfluous; the moments of the unfortunate count were numbered.

With his dying breath he entreated his friend to repair instantly to the castle of Landshort and explain the fatal cause of his not keeping his appointment with his bride. Though not the most ardent of lovers, he was one of the most punctilious of men, and appeared earnestly solicitous that his mission should be speedily and courteously executed. "Unless this is done," said he, "I shall not sleep quietly in my grave." He repeated these last words with peculiar solemnity. A request at a moment so impressive admitted no hesitation. Starkenfaust endeavored to soothe him to calmness, promised faithfully to execute his wish, and gave him his hand in solemn pledge. The dying man pressed it in acknowledgment, but soon lapsed into delirium—raved about his bride, his engagements, his plighted word—ordered his horse, that he might ride to the castle of Landshort, and expired in the fancied act of vaulting into the saddle.

Starkenfaust bestowed a sigh and a soldier's tear on the untimely fate of his comrade and then pondered on the awkward mission he had undertaken. His heart was heavy and his head perplexed; for he was to present himself an unbidden guest among hostile people, and to damp their festivity with tidings fatal to their hopes. Still, there were certain whisperings of curiosity in his heart to see this far-famed beauty of Katzenellenbogen, so cautiously shut up from the world; for he was a passionate admirer of women, and there was a dash of eccentricity and enterprise in his character that made him fond of all singular adventure.

Previous to his departure he made all due arrangements with the holy fraternity of the convent for the funeral solemnities of his friend, who was to be buried in the cathedral of Würzburg near some of his illustrious relatives, and the mourning retinue of the count took charge of his remains.

It is now high time that we should return to the ancient family of Katzenellenbogen, who were impatient for their guest, and still more for their dinner, and to the worthy little baron, whom we left airing himself on the watchtower.

Night closed in, but still no guest arrived. The baron descended from the tower in despair. The banquet, which had been delayed from hour to hour, could no longer be postponed. The meats were already overdone, the cook in an agony, and the whole household had the look of a garrison that had been reduced by famine. The baron was obliged reluctantly to give orders for the feast without the presence of the guest. All were seated at table, and just on the point of commencing, when the sound of a horn from without the gate gave notice of the approach of a stranger. Another long blast filled the old courts of the castle with its echoes, and was answered by the warder from the walls. The baron hastened to receive his future son-in-law.

The drawbridge had been let down, and the stranger was before the gate. He was a tall gallant cavalier, mounted on a black steed. His countenance was pale, but he had a beaming, romantic eye and an air of stately melancholy. The baron was a little mortified that he should have come in this simple, solitary style. His dignity for a moment was ruffled, and he felt disposed to consider it a want of proper respect for the important occasion and the important family with which he was to be connected. He pacified himself, however, with the conclusion that it must have been youthful impatience which had induced him thus to spur on sooner than his attendants.

"I am sorry," said the stranger, "to break in upon you thus unseasonably—"

Here the baron interrupted him with a world of compliments and greetings, for, to tell the truth, he prided himself upon his courtesy and eloquence. The stranger attempted once or twice to stem the torrent of words, but in vain, so he bowed his head and suffered it to flow on. By the time the baron had come to a pause, they had reached the inner court of the castle, and the stranger was again about to speak, when he was once more interrupted by the appearance of the female part of the family, leading forth the shrinking and blushing bride. He gazed on her for a moment as one entranced; it seemed as if his whole soul beamed forth in the gaze and rested upon that lovely form. One of the maiden aunts whispered something into her ear; she made an effort to speak; her moist blue eyes were timidly raised, gave a shy glance of inquiry on the stranger, and were cast again to the ground. The words died away, but there was a sweet smile playing about her lips, and a soft dimpling of the cheek that showed her glance had not been unsatisfactory. It was impossible for a girl of the fond age of eighteen, highly predisposed for love and matrimony, not to be pleased with so gallant a cavalier.

The late hour at which the guest had arrived left no time

for parley. The baron was peremptory, and deferred all particular conversation until the morning, and led the way to the untasted banquet.

It was served up in the great hall of the castle. Around the walls hung the hard-favored portraits of the heroes of the house of Katzenellenbogen, and the trophies which they had gained in the field, and in the chase. Hacked corselets, splintered jousting spears, and tattered banners were mingled with the spoils of sylvan warfare: the jaws of the wolf and the tusks of the boar grinned horribly among crossbows and battle axes, and a huge pair of antlers branched immediately over the head of the youthful bridegroom.

The cavalier took but little notice of the company or the entertainment. He scarcely tasted the banquet, but seemed absorbed in admiration of his bride. He conversed in a low tone that could not be overheard, for the language of love is never loud; but where is the female ear so dull that it cannot catch the softest whisper of the lover? There was a mingled tenderness and gravity in his manner that appeared to have a powerful effect upon the young lady. Her color came and went as she listened with deep attention. Now and then she made some blushing reply, and when his eye was turned away, she would steal a sidelong glance at his romantic countenance, and heave a gentle sigh of tender happiness. It was evident that the young couple were completely enamored. The aunts, who were deeply versed in the mysteries of the heart, declared that the couple had fallen in love with each other at first sight.

The feast went on merrily, or at least noisily, for the guests were all blessed with those keen appetites that attend upon light purses and mountain air. The baron told his best and longest stories, and never had he told them so well or with such great effect. If there was anything marvelous, his auditors were lost in astonishment; and if anything facetious, they were sure to laugh exactly in the right place. The baron, it is true, like most great men, was too dignified to utter any joke but a dull one; it was always enforced, however, by a bumper of excellent Hochheimer, and even a dull joke at one's own table, served up with jolly old wine, is irresistible. Many good things were said by poorer and keener wits that would not bear repeating, except on similar occasions; many sly speeches whispered into ladies' ears that almost convulsed them with suppressed laughter; and a song or two roared out by a poor but merry and broad-faced cousin of the baron that absolutely made the maiden aunts hold up their fans.

Amidst all this revelry the stranger guest maintained a most singular and unseasonable gravity. His countenance assumed a deeper cast of dejection as the evening advanced, and, as strange as it may appear, even the baron's jokes seemed only to render him the more melancholy. At times he was lost in thought, and at times there was a perturbed and restless wandering of the eye that bespoke a mind but ill at ease. His conversations with the bride became more and more earnest and mysterious. Lowering clouds began to steal over the fair serenity of her brow, and tremors to run through her tender frame.

All this could not escape the notice of the company. Their joy was chilled by the unaccountable gloom of the bridegroom; their spirits were infected; whispers and glances were interchanged, accompanied by shrugs and dubious shakes of the head. The song and the laugh grew less and less frequent: there were dreary pauses in the conversation, which were at length succeeded by wild tales and supernatural legends. One dismal story produced another still more dismal, and the baron nearly frightened some of the ladies into hysterics with the history of the goblin horseman that carried away the fair Leonora—a dreadful story which has since been put into excellent verse, and is read and believed by all the world.

The bridegroom listened to this tale with profound attention. He kept his eyes steadily fixed on the baron, and, as the story drew to a close, began gradually to rise from his seat, growing taller and taller, until in the baron's entranced eye he seemed almost to tower into a giant. The moment the tale was finished he heaved a deep sigh and took a solemn farewell of the company. They were all amazement. The baron was perfectly thunderstruck.

"What! Going to leave the castle at midnight?" Why,

everything was prepared for his reception; a chamber was ready for him if he wished to retire.

The stranger shook his head mournfully and mysteriously. "I must lay my head in a different chamber tonight."

There was something in this reply and the tone in which it was uttered that made the baron's heart misgive him; but he rallied his forces and repeated his hospitable entreaties.

The stranger shook his head silently, but positively, at every offer, and, waving his farewell to the company, stalked slowly out of the hall. The maiden aunts were absolutely petrified; the bride hung her head, and a tear stole to her eye.

The baron followed the stranger to the great court of the castle, where the black charger stood pawing the earth and snorting with impatience. When they had reached the portal, whose deep archway was dimly lighted by a cresset, the stranger paused, and addressed the baron in a hollow tone of voice, which the vaulted roof rendered still more sepulchral.

"Now that we are alone," said he, "I will impart to you the reason of my going. I have a solemn, an indispensable engagement—"

"Why," said the baron, "cannot you send someone in your place?"

"It admits of no substitute. I must attend it in person; I must away to Würzburg cathedral—"

"Ay," said the baron, plucking up spirit, "but not until tomorrow—tomorrow you shall take your bride there."

"No! No!" replied the stranger, with tenfold solemnity. "My engagement is with no bride—the worms! The worms expect me! I am a dead man—I have been slain by robbers—my body lies at Würzburg—at midnight I am to be buried—the grave is waiting for me—I must keep my appointment!"

He sprang onto his black charger and dashed over the drawbridge, and the clattering of his horse's hoofs was lost in the whistling of the night blast.

The baron returned to the hall in the utmost consternation, and related what had passed. Two ladies fainted outright; others sickened at the idea of having banqueted with a specter. It was the opinion of some that this might be the wild huntsman, famous in German legend. Some talked of mountain sprites, of wood demons, and of other supernatural beings with which the good people of Germany have been so grievously harassed since time immemorial. One of the poor relations ventured to suggest that it might be some sportive evasion of the young cavalier, and that the very gloominess of the caprice seemed to accord with so melancholy a personage. This, however, drew on him the indignation of the whole company, and especially of the baron, who looked upon him as little better than an infidel; so that he was fain to abjure his heresy as speedily as possible and come into the faith of the true believers.

But, whatever may have been the doubts entertained, they were completely put to an end by the arrival next day of regular missives confirming the intelligence of the young count's murder and his interment in Würzburg cathedral.

The dismay at the castle may well be imagined. The baron shut himself up in his chamber. The guests, who had come to rejoice with him, could not think of abandoning him in his distress. They wandered about the courts or collected in groups in the hall, shaking their heads and shrugging their shoulders at the troubles of so good a man, and sat longer than ever at table, and ate and drank more stoutly than ever, by way of keeping up their spirits. But the situation of the widowed bride was the most pitiable. To have lost a husband before she had even embraced him—and such a husband! If the very specter could be so gracious and noble, what must have been the living man? She filled the house with lamentations.

On the night of the second day of her widowhood, she had retired to her chamber, accompanied by one of her aunts, who insisted on sleeping with her. The aunt, who was one of the best tellers of ghost stories in all Germany, had just been recounting one of her longest, and had fallen asleep in the very midst of it. The chamber was remote and overlooked a small garden. The niece lay pensively gazing at the beams of the rising moon as they trembled on the leaves of an aspen tree before the lattice. The castle clock had just tolled midnight when a soft strain of music stole up from the garden. She rose hastily from her bed and stepped lightly to the window. A tall figure stood among the shadows of the trees. As it raised its head, a beam of moonlight fell upon the countenance. Heaven and earth! She beheld the Specter Bridegroom! A loud shriek at that moment burst upon her ear, and her aunt, who had been awakened by the music and had followed her silently to the window, fell into her arms. When she looked again, the specter had disappeared.

Of the two females, the aunt now required the most soothing, for she was perfectly beside herself with terror. As to the young lady, there was something even in the specter of her lover that seemed endearing. There was still the semblance of manly beauty, and, though the shadow of a man is but little calculated to satisfy the affections of a lovesick girl, yet where the substance is not to be had, even that is consoling. The aunt declared she would never sleep in that chamber again; the niece, for once, was refractory, and declared as strongly that she would sleep in no other in the castle. The consequence was, that she had to sleep in it alone; but she drew a promise from her aunt not to relate the story of the specter, lest she should be denied the only melancholy pleasure left her on earth—that of inhabiting the chamber over which the guardian shade of her lover kept its nightly vigils.

How long the good old lady would have observed this promise is uncertain, for she dearly loved to talk of the marvelous, and there is a triumph in being the first to tell a frightful story; it is, however, still quoted in the neighborhood as a memorable instance of female secrecy that she kept it to herself for a whole week, when she was suddenly absolved from all further restraint by intelligence brought to the breakfast table one morning that the young lady was not to be found. Her room was empty—the bed had not been slept in—the window was open and the bird had flown!

The astonishment and concern with which the intelligence was received can only be imagined by those who have witnessed the agitation which the mishaps of a great man cause among his friends. Even the poor relations paused for a moment from the indefatigable labors of the trencher, when the aunt, who had at first been struck speechless, wrung her hands and shrieked out, "The goblin! She goblin! She's been carried away by the goblin!"

In a few words she related the fearful scene of the garden, and concluded that the specter must have carried off his bride. Two of the domestics corroborated the opinion, for they had heard the clattering of a horse's hoofs down the mountain about midnight, and had no doubt that it was the specter on his black charger bearing her away to the tomb. All present were struck with the direful probability, for events of the kind are extremely common in Germany, as many well-authenticated histories bear witness.

What a lamentable situation was that of the poor baron! What a heartrending dilemma for a fond father and a member of the great family of Katzenellenbogen! His only daughter had either been rapped away to the grave, or he was to have some wood demon for a son-in-law, and perchance a troop of goblin grandchildren. As usual, he was completely bewildered, and all the castle in an uproar. The men were ordered to take horse and scour every road and path and glen of the Odenwald. The baron himself had just drawn on his jackboots, girded on his sword, and was about to mount his steed to sally forth on the doubtful quest, when he was brought to a pause by a new apparition. A lady was seen approaching the castle mounted on a palfrey, attended by a cavalier on horseback. She galloped up to the gate, sprang from her horse, and, falling at the baron's feet, embraced his knees. It was his lost daughter, and her companion—the Specter Bridegroom! The baron was astounded. He looked at his daughter, then at the specter, and almost doubted the evidence of his senses. The latter, too, was wonderfully improved in his appearance since his visit to the world of spirits. His dress was splendid, and set off a noble figure of manly symmetry. He was no longer pale and melancholy. His fine countenance was flushed with the glow of youth, and joy rioted in his large dark eyes.

The mystery was soon cleared up. The cavalier (for, in truth, as you must have known all the while, he was no goblin) announced himself as Sir Herman Von Starkenfaust. He related his adventure with the young count. He told how he had hastened to the castle to deliver the unwelcome tidings, but that the eloquence of the baron had interrupted him in every attempt to tell his tale. How the sight of the bride had completely captivated him and that to pass a few hours near her, he had tacitly suffered the mistake to continue. How he had been sorely perplexed in what way to make a decent retreat, until the baron's goblin stories had suggested his eccentric exit. How, fearing the feudal hostility of the family, he had repeated his visits by stealth—had haunted the garden beneath the young lady's window—had wooed—had won—had borne away in triumph—and, in a word, had wedded the fair.

Under any other circumstances the baron would have been inflexible, for he was tenacious of paternal authority and devoutly obstinate in all family feuds; but he loved his daughter; he had lamented her as lost; he rejoiced to find her still alive; and, though her husband was of a hostile house, yet, thank heaven, he was not a goblin. There was something, it must be acknowledged, that did not exactly accord with his notions of strict veracity in the joke the knight had passed upon him of his being a dead man; but several old friends present, who had served in the wars, assured him that every stratagem was excusable in love, and that the cavalier was entitled to especial privilege, having lately served as a trooper.

Matters, therefore, were happily arranged. The baron pardoned the young couple on the spot. The revels at the castle were resumed. The poor relations overwhelmed this new member of the family with loving kindness; he was so gallant, so generous—and so rich. The aunts, it is true, were somewhat scandalized that their system of strict seclusion and passive obedience should be so badly exemplified, but attributed it all to their negligence in not having the windows grated. One of them was particularly mortified at having her marvelous story marred, and that the only specter she had ever seen should turn out a counterfeit; but the niece seemed perfectly happy at having found him substantial flesh and blood. And so the story ends.

From *TALES OF A TRAVELLER: STRANGE STORIES BY A NERVOUS GENTLEMAN*

A HUNTING DINNER

I WAS ONCE AT A HUNTING DINNER, GIVEN by a worthy foxhunting old baronet, who kept Bachelor's Hall in jovial style, in an ancient rook-haunted family mansion, in one of the middle counties. He had been a devoted admirer of the fair sex in his young days; but having traveled much, studied women in various countries with distinguished success, and returned home profoundly instructed, as he supposed, in the ways of woman, and a perfect master of the art of pleasing, he had the mortification of being jilted by a boarding-school girl, who was scarcely versed in the accidence of love.

The baronet was completely overcome by such an incredible defeat; retired from the world in disgust, put himself under the government of his housekeeper, and took to foxhunting like a perfect Jehu. Whatever poets may say to the contrary, a man will grow out of love as he grows old; and a pack of foxhounds may chase out of his heart even the memory of a boarding-school goddess. The baronet was when I saw him as merry and mellow an old bachelor as ever followed a hound; and the love he had once felt for one woman had spread itself over the whole gender; so that there was not a pretty face in the whole country round but came in for a share.

The dinner was prolonged till a late hour; for our host having no ladies in his household to summon us to the drawing room, the bottle maintained its true bachelor sway, unrivaled by its potent enemy the teakettle. The old hall in which we dined echoed to bursts of robustious foxhunting merriment, that made the ancient antlers shake on the walls. By degrees, however, the wine and wassail of mine host began to operate upon bodies already a little jaded by the chase. The choice spirits that flashed up at the beginning of the dinner, sparkled for a time, then gradually went out one after another, or only emitted now and then a faint gleam from the socket.

Some of the briskest talkers, who had given tongue so

bravely at the first burst, fell fast asleep; and none kept on their way but certain of those long-winded prosers, who, like short-legged hounds, worry on unnoticed at the bottom of conversation, but are sure to be in at the death. Even these at length subsided into silence; and scarcely anything was heard but the nasal communications of two or three veteran masticators, who, having been silent while awake, were indemnifying the company in their sleep.

At length the announcement of tea and coffee in the cedar parlor roused all hands from this temporary torpor. Everyone awoke marvelously renovated, and while sipping the refreshing beverage out of the baronet's old-fashioned hereditary china, began to think of departing for their several homes. But here a sudden difficulty arose. While we had been prolonging our repast, a heavy winter storm had set in, with snow, rain, and sleet, driven by such bitter blasts of wind, that they threatened to penetrate to the very bone.

"It's all in vain," said our hospitable host, "to think of putting one's head out of doors in such weather. So, gentlemen, I hold you my guests for this night at least, and will have your quarters prepared accordingly."

The unruly weather, which became more and more tempestuous, rendered the hospitable suggestion unanswerable. The only question was, whether such an unexpected accession of company, to an already crowded house, would not put the housekeeper to her trumps to accommodate them.

"Pshaw," cried mine host, "did you ever know of a Bachelor's Hall that was not elastic, and able to accommodate twice as many as it could hold?" So out of a good-humored pique the housekeeper was summoned to consultation before us all. The old lady appeared, in her gala suit of faded brocade, which rustled with flurry and agitation, for in spite of mine host's bravado, she was a little perplexed. But in a bachelor's house, and with bachelor guests, these matters are readily managed. There is no lady of the house to stand upon squeamish points about lodging guests in odd holes and corners, and exposing the shabby parts of the establishment. A bachelor's housekeeper is used to shifts and emergencies. After much worrying to and fro, and divers consultations about the red room, and the blue room, and the chintz room, and the damask room, and the little room with the bow window, the matter was finally arranged.

When all this was done, we were once more summoned to the standing rural amusement of eating. The time that had been consumed in dozing after dinner, and in the refreshment and consultation of the cedar parlor, was sufficient, in the opinion of the rosy-faced butler, to engender a reasonable appetite for supper. A slight repast had therefore been tricked up from the residue of dinner, consisting of cold sirloin of beef; hashed venison; a devilled leg of a turkey or so, and a few other of those light articles taken by country gentlemen to ensure sound sleep and heavy snoring.

The nap after dinner had brightened up everyone's wit; and a great deal of excellent humor was expended upon the perplexities of mine host and his housekeeper, by certain married gentlemen of the company, who considered themselves privileged in joking with a bachelor's establishment. From this the banter turned as to what quarters each would find, on being thus suddenly billeted in so antiquated a mansion.

"By my soul," said an Irish captain of dragoons, one of the most merry and boisterous of the party, "by my soul, but I should not be surprised if some of those good-looking gentlefolks that hang along the walls should walk about the rooms of this stormy night; or if I should find the ghost of one of these long-waisted ladies turning into my bed in mistake for her grave in the churchyard."

"Do you believe in ghosts, then?" said a thin, hatchet-faced gentleman, with projecting eyes like a lobster.

I had remarked this last personage throughout dinnertime for one of those incessant questioners, who seem to have a craving, unhealthy appetite in conversation. He never seemed satisfied with the whole of a story; never laughed when others laughed; but always put the joke to the question. He could never enjoy the kernel of the nut, but pestered himself to get more out of the shell.

"Do you believe in ghosts, then?" said the inquisitive gentleman.

"Faith, but I do," replied the jovial Irishman. "I was brought up in the fear and belief of them; we had a banshee in our own family, honey."

"A banshee—and what's that?" cried the questioner.

"Why an old lady ghost that tends upon your real Milesian families, and wails at their window to let them know when some of them are to die."

"A mighty pleasant piece of information," cried an elderly gentleman, with a knowing look and a flexible nose, to which he could give a whimsical twist when he wished to be waggish.

"By my soul, but I'd have you know it's a piece of distinction to be waited upon by a banshee. It's a proof that one has pure blood in one's veins. But, egad, now we're talking of ghosts, there never was a house or a night better fitted than the present for a ghost adventure. Faith, Sir John, haven't you such a thing as a haunted chamber to put a guest in?"

"Perhaps," said the baronet, smiling, "I might accommodate you even on that point."

"Oh, I should like it of all things, my jewel. Some dark oaken room, with ugly woebegone portraits that stare dismally at one, and about which the housekeeper has a power of delightful stories of love and murder. And then a dim lamp, a table with a rusty sword across it, and a specter all in white to draw aside one's curtains at midnight—"

"In truth," said an old gentleman at one end of the table, "you put me in mind of an anecdote—"

"Oh, a ghost story! A ghost story!" was vociferated round the board, everyone edging his chair a little nearer.

The attention of the whole company was now turned upon the speaker. He was an old gentleman, one side of whose face was no match for the other. The eyelid drooped and hung down like an unhinged window shutter. Indeed, the whole side of his head was dilapidated, and seemed like the wing of a house shut up and haunted. I'll warrant that side was well stuffed with ghost stories.

There was a universal demand for the tale.

"Nay," said the old gentleman, "it's a mere anecdote—and a very commonplace one; but such as it is you shall have it. It is a story that I once heard my uncle tell when I was a boy. But whether as having happened to himself or to another, I cannot recollect. But no matter, it's very likely it happened to himself, for he was a man very apt to meet with strange adventures. I have heard him tell of others much more singular. At any rate, we will suppose it happened to himself."

"What kind of man was your uncle?" said the questioning gentleman.

"Why, he was rather a dry, shrewd kind of body; a great traveler, and fond of telling his adventures."

"Pray, how old might he have been when this happened?"

"When what happened?" cried the gentleman with the flexible nose impatiently. "Egad, you have not given anything a chance to happen—come, never mind our uncle's age; let us have his adventures."

The inquisitive gentleman being for the moment silenced, the old gentleman with the haunted head proceeded.

THE ADVENTURE OF MY UNCLE

MANY YEARS SINCE, A LONG TIME BEFORE the French Revolution, my uncle had passed several months at Paris. The English and French were on better terms, in those days, than at present, and mingled cordially together in society. The English went abroad to spend money then, and the French were always ready to help them. They go abroad to save money at present, and that, they can do without French assistance. Perhaps the traveling English were fewer and choicer then, than at present, when the whole nation has broken loose, and inundated the Continent. At any rate, they circulated more readily and currently in foreign society, and my uncle, during his residence in Paris, made many very intimate acquaintances among the French noblesse.

Sometime afterwards, he was making a journey in the wintertime, in that part of Normandy called the Pays de Caux, when, as evening was closing in, he perceived the turrets of an ancient château rising out of the trees of its walled park, each turret with its high conical roof of gray slate, like a candle with an extinguisher on it.

"To whom does that château belong, friend?" cried my uncle to a meager but fiery postillion, who, with tremendous jackboots and tricorner hat, was floundering on before him.

"To Monseigneur the Marquis de ———," said the postillion, touching his hat, partly out of respect to my uncle, and partly out of reverence to the noble name pronounced. My uncle recollected the marquis for a particular friend in Paris, who had often expressed a wish to see him at his paternal château. My uncle was an old traveler, one that knew how to turn things to account. He revolved for a few moments in his mind how agreeable it would be to his friend the marquis to be surprised in this sociable way by a pop visit; and how much more agreeable to himself to get into snug quarters in a château, and have a relish of the marquis's well-known kitchen, and a smack of his superior champagne and burgundy; rather than take up with the miserable lodgment, and miserable fare, of a country inn. In a few minutes, therefore, the meager postillion was cracking his whip like a very devil, or like a true Frenchman, up the long straight avenue that led to the château.

You have no doubt all seen French châteaus, as everybody travels in France nowadays. This was one of the oldest; standing naked and alone, in the midst of a desert of gravel walks and cold stone terraces; with a cold-looking formal garden, cut into angles and rhomboids; and a cold leafless park, divided geometrically by straight alleys; and two or three noseless, cold-looking statues without any clothing; and fountains spouting cold water enough to make one's teeth chatter. At least, such was the feeling they imparted on the wintry day of my uncle's visit; though, in hot summer weather, I'll warrant there was glare enough to scorch one's eyes out.

The smacking of the postillion's whip, which grew more and more intense the nearer they approached, frightened a flight of pigeons out of the dovecote, and rooks out of the roofs; and finally a crew of servants out of the château, with the marquis at their head. He was enchanted to see my uncle; for his château, like the house of our worthy host, had not many more guests at the time than it could accommodate. So he kissed my uncle on each cheek, after the French fashion, and ushered him into the castle.

The marquis did the honors of his house with the urbanity

of his country. In fact, he was proud of his old family château; for part of it was extremely old. There was a tower and chapel that had been built almost before the memory of man; but the rest was more modern; the castle having been nearly demolished during the wars of the League. The marquis dwelled upon this event with great satisfaction, and seemed really to entertain a grateful feeling towards Henry IV, for having thought his paternal mansion worth battering down. He had many stories to tell of the prowess of his ancestors, and several skullcaps, helmets, and crossbows to show; and divers huge boots and buff jerkins, that had been worn by the Leaguers. Above all, there was a two-handled sword, which he could hardly wield; but which he displayed as a proof that there had been giants in his family.

In truth, he was but a small descendant from such great warriors. When you looked at their bluff visages and brawny limbs, as depicted in their portraits, and then at the little marquis, with his spindle shanks; his sallow lanthorn visage, flanked with a pair of powdered earlocks, or ailes de pigeon, that seemed ready to fly away with it; you would hardly believe him to be of the same race. But when you looked at the eyes that sparkled out like a beetle's from each side of his hooked nose, you saw at once that he inherited all the fiery spirit of his forefathers. In fact, a Frenchman's spirit never exhales, however his body may dwindle. It rather rarefies, and grows more inflammable, as the earthly particles diminish;

and I have seen valor enough in a little fiery-hearted French dwarf to have furnished out a tolerable giant.

When once the marquis, as he was wont, put on one of the old helmets that were stuck up in his hall; though his head no more filled it than a dry pea its peasecod; yet his eyes sparkled from the bottom of the iron cavern with the brilliancy of carbuncles, and when he poised the ponderous two-handled sword of his ancestors, you would have thought you saw the doughty little David wielding the sword of Goliath, which was unto him like a weaver's beam.

However, gentlemen, I am dwelling too long on this description of the marquis and his château; but you must excuse me; he was an old friend of my uncle's, and whenever my uncle told the story, he was always fond of talking a great deal about his host.—Poor little marquis! He was one of that handful of gallant courtiers who made such a devoted but hopeless stand in the cause of their sovereign, in the château of the Tuileries, against the irruption of the mob, on the sad tenth of August.

He displayed the valor of a preux French chevalier to the last; flourished feebly his little court sword with a Sa-sa! in face of a whole legion of sansculottes; but was pinned to the wall like a butterfly, by the pike of a poissarde, and his heroic soul was borne up to heaven on his ailes de pigeon.

But all this has nothing to do with my story; to the point then—

When the hour arrived for retiring for the night, my uncle was shown to his room, in a venerable old tower. It was the oldest part of the château, and had in ancient times been the donjon or stronghold; of course the chamber was none of the best. The marquis had put him there, however, because he knew my uncle to be a traveler of taste, and fond of antiquities; and also because the better apartments were already occupied. Indeed, he perfectly reconciled my uncle to his quarters by mentioning the great personages who had once inhabited them, all of whom were in some way or other connected with the family. If you would take his word for it, John Baliol, or, as he called him, Jean de Bailleul, had died of chagrin in this very chamber on hearing of the success of his rival, Robert the Bruce, at the Battle of Bannockburn; and when he added that the Duke de Guise had slept in it during the wars of the League, my uncle was fain to felicitate himself upon being honored with such distinguished quarters.

The night was shrewd and windy, and the chamber none of the warmest. An old, long-faced, long-bodied servant in quaint livery, who attended upon my uncle, threw down an armful of wood beside the fireplace, gave a strange look about the room, and then wished him bon repos, with a grimace and a shrug that would have been suspicious from any other than an old French servant. The chamber had indeed a wild, crazy look, enough to strike anyone who had read romances with apprehension and foreboding. The windows were high and narrow, and had once been loopholes, but had been rudely enlarged, as well as the extreme thickness of the walls would permit; and the ill-fitted casements rattled to every breeze. You would have thought, on a windy night, some of the old Leaguers were tramping and clanking about the apartment in their huge boots and rattling spurs. A door which stood ajar, and like a true French door would stand ajar in spite of every reason and effort to the contrary, opened upon a long, dark corridor, that led the Lord knows whither, and seemed just made for ghosts to air themselves in, when they turned out of their graves at midnight. The wind would spring up into a hoarse murmur through this passage, and creak the door to and fro, as if some dubious ghost were balancing in its mind whether to come in or not. In a word, it was precisely the kind of comfortless apartment that a ghost, if ghost there were in the château, would single out for its favorite lounge.

My uncle, however, though a man accustomed to meet with strange adventures, apprehended none at the time. He made several attempts to shut the door, but in vain. Not that he apprehended anything, for he was too old a traveler to be daunted by a wild-looking apartment; but the night, as I have said, was cold and gusty, something like the present, and the wind howled about the old turret, pretty much as it does round this old mansion at this moment; and the breeze from the long dark corridor came in as damp and chilly as if from a dungeon. My uncle, therefore, since he could not close the door, threw a quantity of wood onto the fire, which soon sent up a flame in the great wide-mouthed chimney that illumined the whole chamber, and made the shadow of the tongs on the opposite wall look like a long-legged giant. My uncle now clambered on top of the half score of mattresses which form a French bed, and which stood in a deep recess; then tucking himself snugly in, and burying himself up to the chin in the bedclothes, he lay looking at the fire, and listening to the wind, and chuckling to think how knowingly he had come over his friend the marquis for a night's lodgings: and so he fell asleep.

He had not taken above half of his first nap, when he was awakened by the clock of the château, in the turret over his chamber, which struck midnight. It was just such an old clock as ghosts are fond of. It had a deep, dismal tone, and struck so slowly and tediously that my uncle thought it would never have done. He counted and counted till he was confident he counted thirteen, and then it stopped.

The fire had burned low, and the blaze of the last bundle of sticks was almost expiring, burning in small blue flames, which now and then lengthened up into little white gleams. My uncle lay with his eyes half-closed, and his nightcap drawn almost down to his nose. His fancy was already wandering, and began to mingle up the present scene with the crater of Vesuvius, the French opera, the Coliseum at Rome, Dolly's chophouse in London, and all the farrago of noted places with which the brain of a traveler is crammed—in a word, he was just falling asleep.

Suddenly he was aroused by the sound of footsteps that appeared to be slowly pacing along the corridor. My uncle, as I have often heard him say himself, was a man not easily frightened; so he lay quiet, supposing that this might be some other guest; or some servant on his way to bed. The footsteps, however, approached the door; the door gently opened; whether of its own accord, or whether pushed open, my uncle could not distinguish—a figure all in white glided in. It was a female, tall and stately in person, and of a most commanding air. Her dress was of an ancient fashion, ample in volume and sweeping the floor. She walked up to the fireplace without regarding my uncle; who raised his nightcap with one hand, and stared earnestly at her. She remained for some time standing by the fire, which flashing up at intervals cast blue and white gleams of light that enabled my uncle to remark her appearance minutely.

Her face was ghastly pale, and perhaps rendered still more so by the bluish light of the fire. It possessed beauty, but its beauty was saddened by care and anxiety. There was the look of one accustomed to trouble, but of one whom trouble could not cast down nor subdue; for there was still the predominating air of proud, unconquerable resolution. Such, at least, was the opinion formed by my uncle, and he considered himself a great physiognomist.

The figure remained, as I said, for some time by the fire, putting out first one hand, then the other, then each foot, alternately, as if warming itself; for your ghosts, if ghost it really was, are apt to be cold. My uncle furthermore remarked that it wore high-heeled shoes, after an ancient fashion, with paste or diamond buckles, that sparkled as though they were alive. At length the figure turned gently round, casting a glassy look about the apartment, which, as it passed over my uncle, made his blood run cold, and chilled the very marrow in his bones. It then stretched its arms toward heaven, clasped its hands, and wringing them in a supplicating manner, glided slowly out of the room.

My uncle lay for some time meditating on this visitation, for (as he remarked when he told me the story) though a man of firmness, he was also a man of reflection, and did not reject a thing because it was out of the regular course of events. However, being, as I have before said, a great traveler, and accustomed to strange adventures, he drew his nightcap resolutely over his eyes, turned his back to the door, hoisted the bedclothes high over his shoulders, and gradually fell asleep.

How long he slept he could not say, when he was awakened by the voice of someone at his bedside. He turned round and beheld the old French servant, with his earlocks in tight buckles on each side of a long, lanthorn face, on which habit had deeply wrinkled an everlasting smile. He made a thousand grimaces and asked a thousand pardons for disturbing monsieur, but the morning was considerably advanced. While my uncle was dressing, he called vaguely to mind the visitor of the preceding night. He asked the ancient domestic what lady was in the habit of rambling about this part of the château at night. The old valet shrugged his shoulders as high as his head, laid one hand on his chest, threw open the other with every finger extended; made a most whimsical grimace, which he meant to be complimentary, and said it was not for him to know anything of les braves fortunes of monsieur.

My uncle saw there was nothing satisfactory to be learned in this quarter. After breakfast he was walking with the marquis through the modern apartments of the château; sliding over the well-waxed floors of silken saloons, amidst furniture rich in gilding and brocade; until they came to a long picture gallery, containing many portraits, some in oil and some in chalks.

Here was an ample field for the eloquence of his host, who had all the family pride of a nobleman of the ancient regime. There was not a grand name in Normandy, and hardly one in France, that was not, in some way or other, connected with his house. My uncle stood listening with inward impatience, resting sometimes on one leg, sometimes on the other, as the little marquis descanted, with his usual fire and vivacity, on the achievements of his ancestors, whose portraits hung along the wall; from the martial deeds of the stern warriors in steel, to the gallantries and intrigues of the blue-eyed gentlemen, with fair smiling faces, powdered earlocks, laced ruffles, and pink and blue silk coats and breeches; not forgetting the conquests of the lovely shepherdesses, with hoop petticoats and waists no thicker than an hour glass, who appeared ruling over their sheep and their swains with dainty crooks decorated with fluttering ribbons.

In the midst of his friend's discourse my uncle's eyes rested on a full-length portrait, which struck him as being the very counterpart of his visitor of the preceding night.

"Methinks," said he, pointing to it, "I have seen the original of this portrait."

"Pardonnez moi," replied the marquis politely, "that can hardly be, as the lady has been dead more than a hundred years. That was the beautiful Duchess de Longueville, who figured during the minority of Louis the Fourteenth."

"And was there anything remarkable in her history?"

Never was question more unlucky. The little marquis immediately threw himself into the attitude of a man about to tell a long story. In fact, my uncle had pulled upon himself the whole history of the civil war of the Fronde, in which the beautiful duchess had played so distinguished a part. Turenne, Coligni, Mazarin, were called up from their graves to grace his narration; nor were the affairs of the Barricadoes, nor the chivalry of the Pertcocheres forgotten. My uncle began to wish himself a thousand leagues off from the marquis and his merciless memory, when suddenly the little man's recollections took a more interesting turn. He was relating the imprisonment of the Duke de Longueville, with the Princes Condé and Conti, in the château of Vincennes, and the ineffectual efforts of the duchess to rouse the sturdy Normans to their rescue. He had come to that part where she was invested by the royal forces in the château of Dieppe, and in imminent danger of falling into their hands.

"The spirit of the duchess," proceeded the marquis, "rose with her trials. It was astonishing to see so delicate and beautiful a being buffet so resolutely with hardships. She determined on a desperate means of escape. One dark unruly night, she issued secretly out of a small postern gate of the castle, which the enemy had neglected to guard. She was followed by her female attendants, a few domestics, and some gallant cavaliers who still remained faithful to her fortunes. Her object was to gain a small port about two leagues distant, where she had privately provided a vessel for her escape in case of emergency.

"The little band of fugitives were obliged to perform the distance on foot. When they arrived at the port, the wind was high and stormy, the tide contrary, the vessel anchored far off in the road, and no means of getting on board, but by a fishing shallop that lay tossing like a cockleshell on the edge of the surf. The duchess determined to risk the attempt. The seamen endeavored to dissuade her, but the imminence of her danger onshore, and the magnanimity of her spirit urged her on. She had to be borne to the shallop in the arms of a mariner. Such was the violence of the wind and waves that he faltered, lost his foothold, and let his precious burden fall into the sea.

"The duchess was nearly drowned; but partly through her own struggles, partly by the exertions of the seamen, she got to land. As soon as she had a little recovered strength, she insisted on renewing the attempt. The storm, however, had by this time become so violent as to set all efforts at defiance. To delay was to be discovered and taken prisoner. As the only resource left, she procured horses; mounted with her female attendants en croupe behind the gallant gentlemen who accompanied her; and scoured the country to seek some temporary asylum.

"While the duchess," continued the marquis, laying his forefinger on my uncle's breast to arouse his flagging attention, "while the duchess, poor lady, was wandering amid the tempest in this disconsolate manner, she arrived at this château. Her approach caused some uneasiness; for the clattering of a troop of horses, at dead of night, up the avenue of a lonely château, in those unsettled times, and in a troubled part of the country, was enough to occasion alarm.

"A tall, broad-shouldered chasseur, armed to the teeth, galloped ahead, and announced the name of the visitor. All uneasiness was dispelled. The household turned out with flambeaux to receive her, and never did torches gleam on a more weather-beaten, travel-stained band than came tramping into the court. Such pale, careworn faces, such bedraggled dresses as the poor duchess and her females presented, each seated behind her cavalier; while half-drenched, half-drowsy pages and attendants seemed ready to fall from their horses with sleep and fatigue.

"The duchess was received with a hearty welcome by my ancestors. She was ushered into the hall of the château, and the fires soon crackled and blazed to cheer herself and her train; and every spit and stewpan was put in requisition to prepare ample refreshments for the wayfarers.

"She had a right to our hospitalities," continued the little marquis, drawing himself up with a slight degree of stateliness, "for she was related to our family. I'll tell you how it was. Her father, Henry de Bourbon, Prince of Condé—"

"But did the duchess pass the night in the château?" said my uncle rather abruptly, terrified at the idea of getting involved in one of the marquis's genealogical discussions.

"Oh, as to the duchess, she was put into the apartment you occupied last night; which, at that time, was a kind of state apartment. Her followers were quartered in the chambers opening upon the neighboring corridor, and her favorite page slept in an adjoining closet. Up and down the corridor walked the great chasseur, who had announced her arrival, and who acted as a kind of sentinel or guard. He was a dark, stern, powerful-looking fellow, and as the light of a lamp in the corridor fell upon his deeply marked face and sinewy form, he seemed capable of defending the castle with his single arm.

"It was a rough, rude night; about this time of the year. Apropos—now I think of it, last night was the anniversary of her visit. I may well remember the precise date, for it was a night not to be forgotten by our house. There is a singular tradition concerning it in our family." Here the marquis hesitated, and a cloud seemed to gather about his bushy eyebrows. "There is a tradition—that a strange occurrence took place that night—a strange, mysterious, inexplicable occurrence."

Here he checked himself and paused.

"Did it relate to that lady?" inquired my uncle eagerly.

"It was past the hour of midnight," resumed the marquis, "when the whole château—"

Here he paused again—my uncle made a movement of anxious curiosity.

"Excuse me," said the marquis—a slight blush streaking his sullen visage. "There are some circumstances connected with our family history which I do not like to relate. That was a rude period. A time of great crimes among great men: for you know high blood, when it runs wrong, will not run tamely like blood of the canaille—poor lady! But I have a little family pride, that—excuse me—we will change the subject if you please."

My uncle's curiosity was piqued. The pompous and magnificent introduction had led him to expect something wonderful in the story to which it served as a kind of avenue. He had no idea of being cheated out of it by a sudden fit of unreasonable squeamishness. Besides, being a traveler, in quest of information, he considered it his duty to inquire into everything.

The marquis, however, evaded every question.

"Well," said my uncle a little petulantly, "whatever you may think of it, I saw that lady last night."

The marquis stepped back and gazed at him with surprise.

"She paid me a visit in my bedchamber."

The marquis pulled out his snuffbox with a shrug and a smile; taking it no doubt for an awkward piece of English pleasantry, which politeness required him to be charmed with. My uncle went on gravely, however, and related the whole circumstance. The marquis heard him through with profound attention, holding his snuffbox unopened in his hand. When the story was finished, he tapped on the lid of his box deliberately; took a long sonorous pinch of snuff—

"Bah!" said the marquis, and walked toward the other end of the gallery.

Here the narrator paused. The company waited for some time for him to resume his narrative; but he continued silent.

"Well," said the inquisitive gentleman, "and what did your uncle say then?"

"Nothing," replied the other.

"And what did the marquis say farther?"

"Nothing."

"And is that all?"

"That is all," said the narrator, filling a glass of wine.

"I surmise," said the shrewd old gentleman with the waggish nose. "I surmise it was the old housekeeper walking her rounds to see that all was right."

"Bah!" said the narrator. "My uncle was too much accustomed to strange sights not to know a ghost from a housekeeper!"

There was a murmur round the table, half of merriment, half of disappointment. I was inclined to think the old gentleman had really an afterpart of his story in reserve; but he sipped his wine and said nothing more; and there was an odd expression about his dilapidated countenance that left me in doubt whether he were in drollery or earnest.

"Egad," said the knowing gentleman with the flexible nose, "this story of your uncle puts me in mind of one that used to be told of an aunt of mine, by the mother's side; though, I don't know that it will bear a comparison; as the good lady was not quite so prone to meet with strange adventures. But at any rate, you shall have it."

THE ADVENTURE OF MY AUNT

My aunt was a lady of large frame, strong mind, and great resolution; she was what might be termed a very manly woman. My uncle was a thin, puny little man, very meek and acquiescent, and no match for my aunt. It was observed that he dwindled and dwindled gradually away, from the day of his marriage. His wife's powerful mind was too much for him; it wore him out. My aunt, however, took all possible care of him, had half the doctors in town to prescribe for him, made him take all their prescriptions, *willy-nilly*, and dosed him with physic enough to cure a whole hospital. All was in vain. My uncle grew worse and worse the more dosing and nursing he underwent, until in the end he added another to the long list of matrimonial victims, who have been killed with kindness.

"And was it his ghost that appeared to her?" asked the inquisitive gentleman, who had questioned the former storyteller.

"You shall hear," replied the narrator, and he continued:

My aunt took on mightily for the death of her poor dear husband! Perhaps she felt some compunction at having given him so much physic, and nursed him into his grave. At any rate, she did all that a widow could do to honor his memory. She spared no expense in either the quantity or quality of her mourning weeds; she wore a miniature of him about her neck, as large as a little sundial; and she had a full-length portrait of him always hanging in her bedchamber. All the world extolled her conduct to the skies; and it was determined, that a woman who behaved so well to the memory of one husband, deserved soon to get another.

It was not long after this that she went to take up her residence in an old country seat in Derbyshire, which had long been in the care of merely a steward and housekeeper. She took most of her servants with her, intending to make it her principal abode. The house stood in a lonely, wild part of the country among the gray Derbyshire hills; with a murderer hanging in chains on a bleak height in full view.

The servants from town were half-frightened out of their wits, at the idea of living in such a dismal, pagan-looking place; especially when they got together in the servants' hall in the evening, and compared notes on all the hobgoblin stories they had picked up in the course of the day. They were afraid to venture alone about the forlorn black-looking chambers. The ladies' maid, who was troubled with nerves, declared she could never sleep alone in such a "gashly, rummaging old building;" and the footman, who was a kindhearted young fellow, did all in his power to cheer her up.

My aunt, herself, seemed to be struck with the lonely appearance of the house. Before she went to bed, therefore, she examined well the fastenings of the doors and windows, locked up the plate with her own hands, and carried the keys, together with a little box of money and jewels, to her own room; for she was a notable woman, and always saw to all things herself. Having put the keys under her pillow, and dismissed her maid, she sat by her toilet arranging her hair; for, being, in spite of her grief for my uncle, rather a buxom widow, she was a little particular about her person. She sat for a little while looking at her face in the glass, first on one side, then on the other, as ladies are apt to do, when they would ascertain if they have been in good looks; for a roystering country squire of the neighborhood, with whom she had flirted when a girl, had called that day to welcome her to the country.

All of a sudden she thought she heard something move behind her. She looked hastily round, but there was nothing to be seen. Nothing but the grimly painted portrait of her poor dear man, which had been hung against the wall. She gave a heavy sigh to his memory, as she was accustomed to do, whenever she spoke of him in company; and went on adjusting her nightdress. Her sigh was re-echoed; or answered by a long-drawn breath. She looked round again, but no one was to be seen. She ascribed these sounds to the wind, oozing through the rat holes of the old mansion; and proceeded leisurely to put her hair in papers, when, all at once, she thought she perceived one of the eyes of the portrait move.

"The back of her head being towards it!" said the storyteller with the ruined head, giving a knowing wink on the sound side of his visage. "Good!"

"Yes, sir!" replied dryly the narrator. "Her back being towards the portrait, but her eye fixed on its reflection in the glass."

Well, as I was saying, she perceived one of the eyes of the portrait move. So strange a circumstance, as you may well suppose, gave her a sudden shock. To assure herself cautiously of the fact, she put one hand to her forehead, as if rubbing it; peeped through her fingers, and moved the candle with the other hand. The light of the taper gleamed on the eye, and was reflected from it. She was sure it moved. Nay, more, it seemed to give her a wink, as she had sometimes known her husband to do when living! It struck a momentary chill to her heart; for she was a lone woman, and felt herself fearfully situated.

The chill was but transient. My aunt, who was almost as resolute a personage as your uncle, sir (turning to the old storyteller), became instantly calm and collected. She went on adjusting her dress. She even hummed a favorite air, and did not make a single false note. She casually overturned a dressing box; took a candle and picked up the articles leisurely, one by one, from the floor, pursued a rolling pincushion that was making the best of its way under the bed; then opened the door; looked for an instant into the corridor, as if in doubt whether to go; and then walked quietly out.

She hastened downstairs, ordered the servants to arm themselves with the first weapons that came to hand, placed herself at their head, and returned almost immediately.

Her hastily levied army presented a formidable force. The steward had a rusty blunderbuss; the coachman a loaded whip; the footman a pair of horse pistols; the cook a huge chopping knife, and the butler a bottle in each hand. My aunt led the van with a red-hot poker; and, in my opinion, she was the most formidable of the party. The waiting maid brought up the rear, dreading to stay alone in the servants' hall, smelling to a broken bottle of volatile salts, and expressing her terror of the ghosteses.

"Ghosts!" said my aunt resolutely. "I'll singe their whiskers for them!"

They entered the chamber. All was as still and undisturbed as when she left it. They approached the portrait of my uncle.

"Pull me down that picture!" cried my aunt.

A heavy groan, and a sound like the chattering of teeth was heard from the portrait. The servants shrank back. The maid uttered a faint shriek, and clung to the footman.

"Instantly!" added my aunt, with a stamp of the foot.

The picture was pulled down, and from a recess behind it, in which had formerly stood a clock, they hauled forth a round-shouldered, black-bearded varlet, with a knife as long as my arm, but trembling all over like an aspen leaf.

"Well, and who was he? No ghost, I suppose!" said the inquisitive gentleman.

"A knight of the post," replied the narrator, "who had been smitten with the worth of the wealthy widow; or rather a marauding Tarquin, who had stolen into her chamber to steal her belongings when all the house should be asleep. In plain terms," continued he, "the vagabond was a loose idle fellow of the neighborhood, who had once been a servant in the house, and had been employed to assist in arranging it for the reception of its mistress. He confessed that he had contrived his hiding place for his nefarious purposes, and had borrowed an eye from the portrait by way of a reconnoitering hole."

"And what did they do with him—did they hang him?" resumed the questioner.

"Hang him? How could they?" exclaimed a beetle-browed barrister with a hawk's nose. "The offence was not capital—no robbery nor assault had been committed—no forcible entry or breaking into the premises—"

"My aunt," said the narrator, "was a woman of spirit, and apt to take the law into her own hands. She had her own notions of cleanliness also. She ordered the fellow to be drawn through the horsepond to cleanse away all offences, and then to be well rubbed down with an oaken towel."

"And what became of him afterwards?" said the inquisitive gentleman.

"I do not exactly know—I believe he was sent on a voyage of improvement to Botany Bay."

"And your aunt," said the inquisitive gentleman. "I'll warrant she took care to make her maid sleep in the room with her after that."

"No, sir, she did better—she gave her hand shortly after to the roystering squire; for she used to observe it was a dismal thing for a woman to sleep alone in the country."

"She was right," observed the inquisitive gentleman, nodding his head sagaciously, "but I am sorry they did not hang that fellow."

It was agreed on all hands that the last narrator had brought his tale to the most satisfactory conclusion; though a country clergyman present regretted that the uncle and aunt, who figured in the different stories, had not been married together. They certainly would have been well matched.

"But I don't see, after all," said the inquisitive gentleman, "that there was any ghost in this last story."

"Oh, if it's ghosts you want, honey," cried the Irish captain of dragoons, "if it's ghosts you want, you shall have a whole regiment of them. And since these gentlemen have been giving the adventures of their uncles and aunts, faith and I'll e'en give you a chapter too, out of my own family history."

THE BOLD DRAGOON; OR THE ADVENTURE OF MY GRANDFATHER

MY GRANDFATHER WAS A BOLD dragoon, for it's a profession, d'ye see, that has run in the family. All my forefathers have been dragoons and died upon the field of honor except myself, and I hope my posterity may be able to say the same; however, I don't mean to be vainglorious. Well, my grandfather, as I said, was a bold dragoon, and had served in the Low Countries. In fact, he was one of that very army, which, according to my uncle Toby, "swore so terribly in Flanders." He could swear a good stick himself; and, moreover, was the very man that introduced the doctrine Corporal Trim mentions, of radical heat and radical moisture; or, in other words, the mode of keeping out the damps of ditch water by burnt brandy. Be that as it may, it's nothing to the purport of my story. I only tell it to show you that my grandfather was a man not easily to be humbugged. He had seen service; or, according to his own phrase, "he had seen the devil"—and that's saying everything.

Well, gentlemen, my grandfather was on his way to England, for which he intended to embark at Ostend—bad luck to the place for one where I was kept by storms and headwinds for three long days, and the devil of a jolly companion or pretty face to comfort me. Well, as I was saying, my grandfather was on his way to England, or rather to Ostend—no matter which, it's all the same. So one evening, towards nightfall, he rode jollily into Bruges. Very like you all know Bruges, gentlemen, a strange, old-fashioned Flemish town, once they say a great place for trade and moneymaking, in old times, when the mynheers were in their glory; but almost as large and as empty as an Irishman's pocket at the present day.

Well, gentlemen, it was the time of the annual fair. All Bruges was crowded; and the canals swarmed with Dutch boats, and the streets swarmed with Dutch merchants; and there was hardly any getting along for goods, wares, and merchandises, and peasants in big breeches, and women in half a score of petticoats.

My grandfather rode jollily along in his easy, slashing way, for he was a saucy, sunshiny fellow—staring about him at the motley crowd, and the old houses with gable ends to the street and storks' nests on the chimneys; winking at the ya vrouws who showed their faces at the windows, and joking the women right and left in the street; all of whom laughed and took it in amazing good part; for though he did not know a word of their language, yet he always had a knack of making himself understood among the women.

Well, gentlemen, it being the time of the annual fair, all the town was crowded; every inn and tavern full, and my grandfather applied in vain from one to the other for admittance. At length he rode up to an old rackety inn that looked ready to fall to pieces, and which all the rats would have run away from, if they could have found room in any other house to put their heads. It was just such a strange building as you see in Dutch pictures, with a tall roof that reached up into the clouds; and as many garrets, one over the other, as the seven heavens of Muhammad. Nothing had saved it from tumbling down but a stork's nest on the chimney, which always brings good luck to a house in the Low Countries; and at the very time of my grandfather's arrival, there were two of these long-legged birds of grace standing like ghosts on the chimney top. Faith, but they've kept the house on its legs to this very day; for you may see it anytime you pass through Bruges, as it stands there yet; only it is turned into a brewery—a brewery of strong Flemish beer; at least it was so when I came that way after the Battle of Waterloo.

My grandfather eyed the house curiously as he approached. It might not altogether have struck his fancy, had he not seen in large letters over the door,

HEER VERKOOPT MAN GOEDEN DRANK.

My grandfather had learned enough of the language to know that the sign promised good liquor. "This is the house for me," said he, stopping short before the door.

The sudden appearance of a dashing dragoon was an event in an old inn, frequented only by the peaceful sons of traffic. A rich burgher of Antwerp, a stately ample man, in a broad Flemish hat, and who was the great man and great patron of the establishment, sat smoking a clean long pipe on one side of the door; a fat little distiller of geneva from Schiedam sat smoking on the other; and the bottle-nosed host stood in the door, and the comely hostess, in crimped cap, beside him; and the hostess's daughter, a plump Flanders lass, with long gold pendants in her ears, was at a side window.

"Humph!" said the rich burgher of Antwerp, with a sulky glance at the stranger.

"Der duyvel!" said the fat little distiller of Schiedam.

The landlord saw with the quick glance of a publican that the new guest was not at all, at all, to the taste of the old ones; and to tell the truth, he did not himself like my grandfather's saucy eye.

He shook his head. "Not a garret in the house but was full."

"Not a garret!" echoed the landlady.

"Not a garret!" echoed the daughter.

The burgher of Antwerp and the little distiller of Schiedam continued to smoke their pipes sullenly, eyed the enemy askance from under their broad hats, but said nothing.

My grandfather was not a man to be browbeaten. He threw the reins onto his horse's neck, tilted his hat to one side, stuck one arm akimbo, slapped his broad thigh with the other hand—

"Faith and troth," said he, "but I'll sleep in this house this very night!"

My grandfather had on a tight pair of buckskins—the slap went to the landlady's heart.

He followed up the vow by jumping off his horse, and making his way past the staring mynheers into the public room. May be you've been in the barroom of an old Flemish inn—faith, but a handsome chamber it was as you'd wish to see; with a brick floor, a great fireplace, with the whole Bible history in glazed tiles; and then the mantelpiece, pitching itself head foremost out of the wall, with a whole regiment of cracked teapots and earthen jugs paraded on it; not to mention half a dozen great delft platters hung about the room by way of pictures; and the little bar in one corner, and the bouncing barmaid inside of it with a red calico cap and yellow eardrops.

My grandfather snapped his fingers over his head, as he cast an eye round the room. "Faith, this is the very house I've been looking after," said he.

There was some farther show of resistance on the part of the garrison, but my grandfather was an old soldier, and an Irishman to boot, and not easily repulsed, especially after he had gotten into the fortress. So he blarney'd the landlord, kissed the landlord's wife, tickled the landlord's daughter, chucked the barmaid under the chin; and it was agreed on all hands that it would be a thousand pities, and a burning shame into the bargain, to turn such a bold dragoon into the streets. So they laid their heads together, that is to say, my grandfather and the landlady, and it was at length agreed to accommodate him with an old chamber that had for some time been shut up.

"Some say it's haunted," whispered the landlord's daughter, "but you're a bold dragoon, and I daresay you don't fear ghosts."

"The devil a bit!" said my grandfather, pinching her plump cheek. "But if I should be troubled by ghosts, I've been to the Red Sea in my time, and have a pleasant way of laying them, my darling!"

And then he whispered something to the girl which made her laugh, and give him a good-humored box on the ear. In short, there was nobody knew better how to make his way among the petticoats than my grandfather.

In a little while, as was his usual way, he took complete

possession of the house, swaggering all over it—into the stable to look after his horse; into the kitchen to look after his supper. He had something to say or do with everyone; smoked with the Dutchmen; drank with the Germans; slapped the men on the shoulders, tickled the women under the ribs. Never since the days of Ally Croaker had such a rattling blade been seen. The landlord stared at him with astonishment; the landlord's daughter hung her head and giggled whenever he came near; and as he turned his back and swaggered along, his tight jacket setting off his broad shoulders and plump buckskins, and his long sword trailing by his side, the maids whispered to one another, "What a proper man!"

At supper my grandfather took command of the table d'hôte as though he had been at home; helped everybody, not forgetting himself; talked with everyone, whether he understood their language or not; and made his way into the intimacy of the rich burgher of Antwerp, who had never been known to be sociable with anyone during his life. In fact, my grandfather revolutionized the whole establishment, and gave it such a rouse, that the very house reeled with it. He outsat everyone at table excepting the little fat distiller of Schiedam, who had sat soaking for a long time before he broke forth; but when he did, he was a very devil incarnate. He took a violent affection for my grandfather; so they sat drinking, and smoking, and telling stories, and singing Dutch and Irish songs, without understanding a word each other said, until the little Hollander was fairly swamped with his own gin and water, and carried off to bed, whooping and hiccuping, and trolling the burden of a Low Dutch love song.

Well, gentlemen, my grandfather was shown to his quarters, up a huge staircase composed of loads of hewn timber; and through long rigmarole passages, hung with blackened paintings of fruit, and fish, and game, and country frolics, and huge kitchens, and portly burgomasters, such as you see about old-fashioned Flemish inns, till at length he arrived at his room.

An old-times chamber it was, sure enough, and crowded with all kinds of trumpery. It looked like an infirmary for decayed and superannuated furniture; where everything diseased and disabled was sent to nurse, or to be forgotten. Or rather, it might have been taken for a general congress of old legitimate movables, where every kind and country had a representative. No two chairs were alike: such high backs and low backs, and leather bottoms and worsted bottoms, and straw bottoms, and no bottoms; and cracked marble tables with curiously carved legs, holding balls in their claws, as though they were going to play at ninepins.

My grandfather made a bow to the motley assemblage as he entered, and having undressed himself, placed his light in the fireplace, asking pardon of the tongs, which seemed to be making love to the shovel in the chimney corner, and whispering soft nonsense into its ear.

The rest of the guests were by this time sound asleep; for your mynheers are huge sleepers. The housemaids, one by one, crept up yawning to their attics, and not a female head in the inn was laid on a pillow that night without dreaming of the bold dragoon.

My grandfather, for his part, got into bed, and drew over him one of those great bags of down, under which they smother a man in the Low Countries; and there he lay, melting between two feather beds, like an anchovy sandwiched between two slices of toast and butter. He was a warm-complexioned man, and this smothering played the very deuce with him. So, sure enough, in a little while it seemed as if a legion of imps were twitching at him and all the blood in his veins was in fever heat.

He lay still, however, until all the house was quiet, excepting the snoring of the mynheers from the different chambers; who answered one another in all kinds of tones and cadences, like so many bullfrogs in a swamp. The quieter the house became, the more unquiet became my grandfather. He waxed warmer and warmer, until at length the bed became too hot to hold him.

"May be the maid had warmed it too much?" said the curious gentleman inquiringly.

"I rather think the contrary," replied the Irishman. "But be that as it may, it grew too hot for my grandfather."

"Faith, there's no standing this any longer," says he; so he jumped out of bed and went strolling about the house.

"What for?" said the inquisitive gentleman.

"Why, to cool himself to be sure," replied the other, "or perhaps to find a more comfortable bed—or perhaps—but no matter what he went for—he never mentioned; and there's no use in taking up our time in conjecturing."

Well, my grandfather had been for some time absent from his room, and was returning, perfectly cool, when just as he reached the door, he heard a strange noise within. He paused and listened. It seemed as if someone was trying to hum a tune in defiance of the asthma. He recollected the report of the room's being haunted; but he was no believer in ghosts. So he pushed the door gently ajar, and peeped in.

Egad, gentlemen, there was a gambol carrying on within enough to have astonished St. Anthony.

By the light of the fire he saw a pale wizen-faced fellow in a long flannel gown and a tall white nightcap with a tassel to it, who sat by the fire, with a bellows under his arm by way of bagpipe, from which he forced the asthmatical music that had bothered my grandfather. As he played, too, he kept twitching about with a thousand strange contortions; nodding his head and bobbing about his tasseled nightcap.

My grandfather thought this very odd, and mighty presumptuous, and was about to demand what business he had to play his wind instruments in another gentleman's quarters, when a new cause of astonishment met his eye. From the opposite side of the room a long-backed, bandy-legged chair, covered with leather, and studded all over in a coxcombical fashion with little brass nails, got suddenly into motion; thrust out first a claw foot, then a crooked arm, and at length, making a leg, slid gracefully up to an easy chair of tarnished brocade, with a hole in its bottom, and led it gallantly out in a ghostly minuet about the floor.

The musician now played fiercer and fiercer, and bobbed his head and his nightcap about like mad. By degrees the dancing mania seemed to seize upon all the other pieces of furniture. The antique, long-bodied chairs paired off in couples and led down a country dance; a three-legged stool danced a hornpipe, though horribly puzzled by its supernumerary leg; while the amorous tongs seized the shovel round the waist, and whirled it about the room in a German waltz. In short, all the movables got into motion, capering about; pirouetting, hands across, right and left, like so many devils, all except a great clothes press, which kept curtsying and curtsying, like a dowager, in one corner, in exquisite time to the music—being either too corpulent to dance or perhaps at a loss for a partner.

My grandfather concluded the latter to be the reason; so, being, like a true Irishman, devoted to women, and at all times ready for a frolic, he bounced into the room, calling to the musician to strike up "Paddy O'Rafferty," capered up to the clothes press and seized upon two handles to lead her out—When, whizz!—the whole revel was at an end. The chairs, tables, tongs, and shovel slunk in an instant as quietly into their places as if nothing had happened; and the musician vanished up the chimney, leaving the bellows behind him in his hurry. My grandfather found himself seated in the middle of the floor, with the clothes press sprawling before him, and the two handles jerked off and in his hands.

"Then after all, this was a mere dream!" said the inquisitive gentleman.

"The devil a bit of a dream!" replied the Irishman. "There never was a truer fact in this world. Faith, I should have liked to see any man tell my grandfather it was a dream."

Well, gentlemen, as the clothes press was a mighty heavy body, and my grandfather likewise, particularly in rear, you may easily suppose two such heavy bodies coming to the ground would make a bit of a noise. Faith, the old mansion shook as though it had mistaken it for an earthquake. The whole garrison was alarmed. The landlord, who slept just below, hurried up with a candle to inquire the cause, but with all his haste his daughter had hurried to the scene of uproar before him. The landlord was followed by the landlady, who was followed by the bouncing barmaid, who was followed by the simpering chambermaids all holding together, as well as they could, such garments as they had first lain hands on; but all in a terrible hurry to see what the devil was to pay in the chamber of the bold dragoon.

My grandfather related the marvelous scene he had witnessed, and the prostrate clothes press, and the broken handles, bore testimony to the fact. There was no contesting such evidence; particularly with a lad of my grandfather's complexion, who seemed able to make good every word either with sword or shillelagh. So the landlord scratched his head and looked silly, as he was apt to do when puzzled. The landlady scratched—no, she did not scratch her head, but she knit her brow, and did not seem half-pleased with the explanation. But the landlady's daughter corroborated it by recollecting that the last person who had dwelled in that chamber was a famous juggler who had died of Saint Vitus's dance, and no doubt had infected all the furniture.

This set all things to rights, particularly when the chambermaids declared that they had all witnessed strange carryings on in that room; and as they declared this "upon their honors," there could not remain a doubt upon the subject.

"And did your grandfather go to bed again in that room?" said the inquisitive gentleman.

"That's more than I can tell. Where he passed the rest of the night was a secret he never disclosed. In fact, though he had seen much service, he was but indifferently acquainted with geography, and apt to make blunders in his travels about inns at night, that it would have puzzled him sadly to account for in the morning."

"Was he ever apt to walk in his sleep?" said the knowing old gentleman.

"Never that I heard of."

THE ADVENTURE OF THE GERMAN STUDENT

ON A STORMY NIGHT, IN THE TEMPEStuous times of the French Revolution, a young German was returning to his lodgings, at a late hour, across the old part of Paris. The lightning gleamed, and the loud claps of thunder rattled through the lofty, narrow streets—but I should first tell you something about this young German.

Gottfried Wolfgang was a young man of good family. He had studied for some time at Göttingen, but being of a visionary and enthusiastic character, he had wandered into those wild and speculative doctrines which have so often bewildered German students. His secluded life, his intense application, and the singular nature of his studies, had an effect on both mind and body. His health was impaired; his imagination diseased. He had been indulging in fanciful speculations on spiritual essences until, like Swedenborg, he had an ideal world of his own around him. He took up a notion, I do not know from what cause, that there was an evil influence hanging over him; an evil genius or spirit seeking to ensnare him and ensure his perdition. Such an idea working on his melancholy temperament produced the most gloomy effects. He became haggard and desponding. His friends discovered the mental malady preying upon him, and determined that the best cure was a change of scene; he was sent, therefore, to finish his studies amidst the splendors and gaieties of Paris.

Wolfgang arrived at Paris at the breaking out of the revolution. The popular delirium at first caught his enthusiastic mind, and he was captivated by the political and philosophical theories of the day: but the scenes of blood which followed shocked his sensitive nature; disgusted him with society and the world, and made him more than ever a recluse. He shut himself up in a solitary apartment in the Pays Latin, the quarter of students. There in a gloomy street not far from the monastic walls of the Sorbonne, he pursued his favorite speculations. Sometimes he spent hours together in the great libraries of Paris, those catacombs of departed authors, rummaging among their hoards of dusty and obsolete works in quest of food for his unhealthy appetite. He was, in a manner, a literary ghoul, feeding in the charnel house of decayed literature.

Wolfgang, though solitary and recluse, was of an ardent temperament, but for a time it operated merely upon his imagination. He was too shy and ignorant of the world to make any advances to the fair sex, but he was a passionate admirer of female beauty, and in his lonely chamber would often lose himself in reveries on forms and faces which he had seen, and his fancy would deck out images of loveliness far surpassing the reality.

While his mind was in this excited and sublimated state, a dream produced an extraordinary effect upon him. It was of a female face of transcendent beauty. So strong was the impression made, that he dreamed of it again and again. It haunted his thoughts by day, his slumbers by night; in fine, he became passionately enamored of this shadow of a dream. This lasted so long, that it became one of those fixed ideas which haunt the minds of melancholy men, and are at times mistaken for madness.

Such was Gottfried Wolfgang, and such his situation at the time I mentioned. He was returning home late one stormy night, through some of the old and gloomy streets of the Marais, the ancient part of Paris. The loud claps of thunder rattled among the high houses of the narrow streets.

He came to the Place de Grève, the square where public executions are performed. The lightning quivered about the pinnacles of the ancient Hôtel de Ville, and shed flickering gleams over the open space in front. As Wolfgang was crossing the square, he shrank back with horror at finding himself close by the guillotine. It was the height of the Reign of Terror, when this dreadful instrument of death stood ever ready, and its scaffold was continually running with the blood of the virtuous and the brave. It had that very day been actively employed in the work of carnage, and there it stood in grim array amidst a silent and sleeping city, waiting for fresh victims.

Wolfgang's heart sickened within him, and he was turning, shuddering, from the horrible engine, when he beheld a shadowy form cowering as it were at the foot of the steps which led up to the scaffold. A succession of vivid flashes of lightning revealed it more distinctly. It was a female figure, dressed in black. She was seated on one of the lower steps of the scaffold, leaning forward, her face hid in her lap, and her long disheveled tresses hanging to the ground, streaming with the rain which fell in torrents. Wolfgang paused. There was something awful in this solitary monument of woe. The female had the appearance of being above the common order. He knew the times to be full of vicissitude, and that many a fair head, which had once been pillowed on down, now wandered houseless. Perhaps this was some poor mourner whom the dreadful axe had rendered desolate, and who sat here heartbroken on the strand of existence, from which all that was dear to her had been launched into eternity.

He approached, and addressed her in the accents of sympathy. She raised her head and gazed wildly at him. What was his astonishment at beholding, by the bright glare of the lightning, the very face which had haunted him in his dreams. It was pale and disconsolate, but ravishingly beautiful.

Trembling with violent and conflicting emotions, Wolfgang again accosted her. He spoke something of her being exposed at such an hour of the night, and to the fury of such a storm, and offered to conduct her to her friends. She pointed to the guillotine with a gesture of dreadful signification.

"I have no friend on earth!" said she.

"But you have a home," said Wolfgang.

"Yes—in the grave!"

The heart of the student melted at the words.

"If a stranger dare make an offer," said he, "without danger of being misunderstood, I would offer my humble dwelling as a shelter; myself as a devoted friend. I am friendless myself in Paris, and a stranger in the land; but if my life could be of service, it is at your disposal, and should be sacrificed before harm or indignity should come to you."

There was an honest earnestness in the young man's manner that had its effect. His foreign accent, too, was in his favor; it showed him not to be a hackneyed inhabitant of Paris. Indeed there is an eloquence in true enthusiasm that is not to be doubted. The homeless stranger confided herself implicitly to the protection of the student.

He supported her faltering steps across the Pont Neuf, and by the place where the statue of Henry IV had been overthrown by the populace. The storm had abated, and the thunder rumbled at a distance. All Paris was quiet; that great volcano of human passion slumbered for a while, to gather fresh strength for the next day's eruption. The student conducted his charge through the ancient streets of the Pays Latin, and by the dusky walls of the Sorbonne to the great, dingy hotel which he inhabited. The old porter who admitted them stared with surprise at the unusual sight of the melancholy Wolfgang with a female companion.

On entering his apartment, the student, for the first time, blushed at the scantiness and indifference of his dwelling. He had but one chamber—an old-fashioned saloon—heavily carved and fantastically furnished with the remains of former magnificence, for it was one of those hotels in the quarter of the Luxembourg Palace which had once belonged to nobility. It was lumbered with books and papers, and all the usual apparatus of a student, and his bed stood in a recess at one end.

When lights were brought, and Wolfgang had a better opportunity of contemplating the stranger, he was more than ever intoxicated by her beauty. Her face was pale, but of a dazzling fairness, set off by a profusion of raven hair that hung clustering about it. Her eyes were large and brilliant, with a singular expression approaching almost to wildness. As far as her black dress permitted her shape to be seen, it was of perfect symmetry. Her whole appearance was highly striking, though she was dressed in the simplest style. The only thing approaching to an ornament which she wore was a broad, black band round her neck, clasped by diamonds.

The perplexity now commenced with the student how to dispose of the helpless being thus thrown upon his protection. He thought of abandoning his chamber to her, and seeking shelter for himself elsewhere. Still he was so fascinated by her charms, there seemed to be such a spell upon his thoughts and senses, that he could not tear himself from her presence. Her manner, too, was singular and unaccountable. She spoke no more of the guillotine. Her grief had abated. The attentions of the student had first won her confidence, and then, apparently, her heart. She was evidently an enthusiast like himself, and enthusiasts soon understand each other.

In the infatuation of the moment Wolfgang avowed his passion for her. He told her the story of his mysterious dream, and how she had possessed his heart before he had even seen her. She was strangely affected by his recital, and acknowledged to have felt an impulse towards him equally unaccountable. It was the time for wild theory and wild actions. Old prejudices and superstitions were done away; everything was under the sway of the "Goddess of Reason." Among other rubbish of the old times, the forms and ceremonies of marriage began to be considered superfluous bonds for honorable minds. Social compacts were the vogue. Wolfgang was too much of a theorist not to be tainted by the liberal doctrines of the day.

"Why should we separate?" said he. "Our hearts are united; in the eye of reason and honor we are as one. What need is there of sordid forms to bind high souls together?"

The stranger listened with emotion; she had evidently received illumination at the same school.

"You have no home nor family," continued he. "Let me be everything to you, or rather let us be everything to one another. If form is necessary, form shall be observed—there is my hand. I pledge myself to you forever."

"Forever?" said the stranger solemnly.

"Forever!" repeated Wolfgang.

The stranger clasped the hand extended to her. "Then I am yours," murmured she, and sank upon his chest.

The next morning the student left his bride sleeping, and sallied forth at an early hour to seek more spacious apartments, suitable to the change in his situation. When he returned, he found the stranger lying with her head hanging over the bed, and one arm thrown over it. He spoke to her, but received no reply. He advanced to awaken her from her uneasy posture. On taking her hand, it was cold—there was no pulsation—her face was pallid and ghastly. In a word, she was a corpse.

Horrified and frantic, he alarmed the house. A scene of confusion ensued. The police were summoned. As the officer of police entered the room, he started back on beholding the corpse.

"Great heaven!" cried he. "How did this woman come here?"

"Do you know anything about her?" said Wolfgang eagerly.

"Do I?" exclaimed the police officer. "She was guillotined yesterday!"

He stepped forward and undid the black collar round the neck of the corpse, and the head rolled onto the floor!

The student burst into a frenzy. "The fiend! The fiend has gained possession of me!" shrieked he. "I am lost forever!"

They tried to soothe him, but in vain. He was possessed with the frightful belief that an evil spirit had reanimated the dead body to ensnare him. He went distracted, and died in a madhouse.

Here the old gentleman with the haunted head finished his narrative.

"And is this really a fact?" said the inquisitive gentleman.

"A fact not to be doubted," replied the other. "I had it from the best authority. The student told it me himself. I saw him in a madhouse at Paris."

THE ADVENTURE OF THE MYSTERIOUS PICTURE

A S ONE STORY OF THE KIND PRODUCES another, and as all the company seemed fully engrossed by the topic, and disposed to bring their relatives and ancestors upon the scene, there is no knowing how many more ghost adventures we might have heard, had not a corpulent old foxhunter, who had slept soundly through the whole, now suddenly awakened, with a loud and long-drawn yawn. The sound broke the charm; the ghosts took to flight as though it had been cockcrow, and there was a universal move for bed.

"And now for the haunted chamber," said the Irish captain, taking his candle.

"Aye, who's to be the hero of the night?" said the gentleman with the ruined head.

"That we shall see in the morning," said the old gentleman with the nose. "Whoever looks pale and grizzly will have seen the ghost."

"Well, gentlemen," said the baronet, "there's many a true thing said in jest. In fact, one of you will sleep in a room tonight—"

"What—a haunted room?"

"A haunted room? I claim the adventure—"

"And I—"

"And I—"

"And I," cried a dozen guests, talking and laughing at the same time.

"No—no," said mine host, "there is a secret about one of my rooms on which I feel disposed to try an experiment. So, gentlemen, none of you shall know who has the haunted chamber, until circumstances reveal it. I will not even know it myself, but will leave it to chance and the allotment of the housekeeper. At the same time, if it will be any satisfaction to you, I will observe, for the honor of my paternal mansion, that there's scarcely a chamber in it but is well worthy of being haunted."

We now separated for the night, and each went to his

allotted room. Mine was in one wing of the building, and I could not but smile at its resemblance in style to those eventful apartments described in the tales of the supper table. It was spacious and gloomy, decorated with lampblack portraits, a bed of ancient damask, with a tester sufficiently lofty to grace a couch of state, and a number of massive pieces of old-fashioned furniture. I drew a great claw-footed armchair before the wide fireplace; stirred up the fire; sat looking into it, and musing upon the odd stories I had heard; until, partly overcome by the fatigue of the day's hunting, and partly by the wine and wassail of mine host, I fell asleep in my chair.

The uneasiness of my position made my slumber troubled, and laid me at the mercy of all kinds of wild and fearful dreams; now it was that my perfidious dinner and supper rose in rebellion against my peace. I was hag-ridden by a fat saddle of mutton; a plum pudding weighed like lead upon my conscience; the merry thought of a capon filled me with horrible suggestions; and a deviled leg of a turkey stalked in all kinds of diabolical shapes through my imagination. In short, I had a violent fit of the nightmare. Some strange indefinite evil seemed hanging over me that I could not avert; something terrible and loathsome oppressed me that I could not shake off. I was conscious of being asleep, and strove to rouse myself, but every effort redoubled the evil; until gasping, struggling, almost strangling, I suddenly sprang bolt upright in my chair, and awoke.

The light on the mantelpiece had burned low, and the wick was divided; there was a great winding sheet made by the dripping wax, on the side towards me. The disordered taper emitted a broad flaring flame, and threw a strong light on a painting over the fireplace, which I had not hitherto observed.

It consisted merely of a head, or rather a face, that appeared to be staring full upon me, and with an expression that was startling. It was without a frame, and at the first glance I could hardly persuade myself that it was not a real face, thrusting itself out of the dark oaken panel. I sat in my chair gazing at it, and the more I gazed, the more it disquieted me. I had never before been affected in the same way by any painting. The emotions it caused were strange and indefinite. They were something like what I have heard ascribed to the eyes of the basilisk; or like that mysterious influence in reptiles termed fascination. I passed my hand over my eyes several times, as if seeking instinctively to brush away this allusion— in vain—they instantly reverted to the picture, and its chilling, creeping influence over my flesh was redoubled.

I looked around the room on other pictures, either to divert my attention, or to see whether the same effect would be produced by them. Some of them were grim enough to produce the effect, if the mere grimness of the painting produced it—no such thing. My eye passed over them all with perfect indifference, but the moment it reverted to this visage over the fireplace, it was as if an electric shock darted through me. The other pictures were dim and faded; but this one protruded from a plain black ground in the strongest relief, and with wonderful truth of coloring. The expression was that of agony—the agony of intense bodily pain; but a menace scowled upon the brow, and a few sprinklings of blood added to its ghastliness. Yet it was not all these characteristics—it was some horror of the mind, some inscrutable antipathy awakened by this picture, which harrowed up my feelings.

I tried to persuade myself that this was chimerical; that my brain was confused by the fumes of mine host's good cheer, and, in some measure, by the odd stories about paintings which had been told at supper. I determined to shake off these vapors of the mind; rose from my chair, and walked about the room; snapped my fingers; rallied myself; laughed aloud. It was a forced laugh, and the echo of it in the old chamber jarred upon my ear. I walked to the window; tried to discern the landscape through the glass. It was pitch-darkness, and howling storm without; and as I heard the wind moan among the trees, I caught a reflection of this accursed visage in the pane of glass, as though it were staring through the window at me. Even the reflection of it was thrilling.

How was this vile nervous fit, for such I now persuaded myself it was, to be conquered? I determined to force myself not to look at the painting but to undress quickly and get into bed. I began to undress, but in spite of every effort I could not keep myself from stealing a glance every now and then at the picture; and a glance was now sufficient to distress me. Even when my back was turned to it, the idea of this strange face behind me, peering over my shoulder, was insufferable. I threw off my clothes and hurried into bed; but still this visage gazed upon me. I had a full view of it from my bed, and for some time could not take my eyes from it. I had grown nervous to a dismal degree.

I put out the light, and tried to force myself to sleep—all in vain! The fire gleaming up a little threw an uncertain light about the room, leaving, however, the region of the picture in deep shadow. What, thought I, if this be the chamber about which mine host spoke as having a mystery reigning over it? I had taken his words merely as spoken in jest; might they have a real import? I looked around. The faintly lighted apartment had all the qualifications requisite for a haunted chamber. It began in my infected imagination to assume strange appearances. The old portraits turned paler and paler, and blacker and blacker; the streaks of light and shadow thrown among the quaint old articles of furniture gave them singular shapes and characters. There was a huge dark clothes press of antique form, gorgeous in brass and lustrous with wax, that began to grow oppressive to me.

Am I then, thought I, indeed, the hero of the haunted room? Is there really a spell laid upon me, or is this all some contrivance of mine host, to raise a laugh at my expense? The idea of being hag-ridden by my own fancy all night, and then bantered on my haggard looks the next day, was intolerable; but the very idea was sufficient to produce the effect, and to render me still more nervous. "Pish," said I, "it can be no such thing." How could my worthy host imagine that I, or any man, would be so worried by a mere picture? It is my own diseased imagination that torments me. I turned in my bed, and shifted from side to side, to try to fall asleep; but all in vain. When one cannot get asleep by lying quiet, it is seldom that tossing about will effect the purpose. The fire gradually went out and left the room in darkness. Still I had the idea of this inexplicable countenance gazing and keeping watch upon me through the darkness. Nay, what was worse, the very darkness seemed to give it additional power, and to multiply its terrors. It was like having an unseen enemy hovering about one in the night. Instead of having one picture now to worry me, I had a hundred. I fancied it in every direction. *And there it is,* thought I, *and there, and there, with its horrible and mysterious expression, still gazing and gazing on me.* No, if I must suffer this strange and dismal influence, it were better to face a single foe, than thus be haunted by a thousand images of it.

Whoever has been in such a state of nervous agitation must know that the longer it continues, the more uncontrollable it grows; the very air of the chamber seemed at length infected by the baleful presence of this picture. I fancied it hovering over me. I almost felt the fearful visage from the wall approaching my face—it seemed breathing upon me. "This is not to be borne," said I, at length, springing out of bed. "I can stand this no longer. I shall only tumble and toss about here all night; make a very specter of myself, and become the hero of the haunted chamber in good earnest. Whatever be the consequence, I'll quit this cursed room, and seek a night's rest elsewhere. They can but laugh at me at all events, and they'll be sure to have the laugh upon me if I pass a sleepless night and show them a haggard and woebegone visage in the morning."

All this was half muttered to myself, as I hastily slipped on my clothes; which having done, I groped my way out of the room, and downstairs to the drawing room. Here, after tumbling over two or three pieces of furniture, I made out to reach a sofa, and stretching myself upon it determined to bivouac there for the night.

The moment I found myself out of the neighborhood of that strange picture, it seemed as if the charm were broken. All its influence was at an end. I felt assured that it was confined to its own dreary chamber, for I had, with a sort of instinctive caution, turned the key when I closed the door. I soon calmed down, therefore, into a state of tranquility; from that into a drowsiness, and finally into a deep sleep; out of which I did not awake, until the housemaid, with her besom and her matin song, came to put the room in order. She stared at finding me stretched upon the sofa; but I presume circumstances of the kind were not uncommon after hunting dinners, in her master's bachelor establishment; for she went on with her song and her work, and took no farther heed of me.

I had an unconquerable repugnance to return to my chamber; so I found my way to the butler's quarters, made my toilet in the best way circumstances would permit, and was among the first to appear at the breakfast table. Our breakfast was a substantial foxhunter's repast, and the company were generally assembled at it. When ample justice had been done to the tea, coffee, cold meats, and humming ale, for all these were furnished in abundance, according to the tastes of the different guests, the conversation began to break out, with all the liveliness and freshness of morning mirth.

"But who is the hero of the haunted chamber? Who has seen the ghost last night?" said the inquisitive gentleman, rolling his lobster eyes about the table.

The question set every tongue in motion; a vast deal of bantering; criticizing of countenances; of mutual accusation and retort took place. Some had drunk deep, and some were unshaven, so that there were suspicious faces enough in the assembly. I alone could not enter with ease and vivacity into the joke. I felt tongue-tied—embarrassed. A recollection of what I had seen and felt the preceding night still haunted my mind.

It seemed as if the mysterious picture still held a thrall upon me. I thought also that our host's eye was turned on me with an air of curiosity. In short, I was conscious that I was the hero of the night, and felt as if everyone might read it in my looks.

The jokes, however, passed over, and no suspicion seemed to attach to me. I was just congratulating myself on my escape, when a servant came in, saying that the gentleman who had slept on the sofa in the drawing room had left his watch under one of the pillows. My repeater was in his hand.

"What!" said the inquisitive gentleman. "Did any gentleman sleep on the sofa?"

"So-ho! So-ho! A hare—a hare!" cried the old gentleman with the flexible nose.

I could not avoid acknowledging the watch, and was rising in great confusion, when a boisterous old squire who sat beside me exclaimed, slapping me on the shoulder, "'Sblood, lad! Thou'rt the man as has seen the ghost!"

The attention of the company was immediately turned to me; if my face had been pale the moment before, it now glowed almost to burning. I tried to laugh, but could only make a grimace; and found all the muscles of my face twitching at sixes and sevens, and totally out of all control.

It takes but little to raise a laugh among a set of foxhunters. There was a world of merriment and joking at my expense; and as I never relished a joke overmuch when it was at my own expense, I began to feel a little nettled. I tried to look cool and calm and to restrain my pique; but the coolness and calmness of a man in a passion are confounded treacherous.

"Gentlemen," said I, with a slight tipping of the chin, and a bad attempt at a smile, "this is all very pleasant"—Ha-ha!—"very pleasant, but I'd have you know, I am as little superstitious as any of you." Ha-ha! "And as to anything like timidity—you may smile, gentlemen, but I trust there is no one here who means to insinuate that. As to a room's being haunted, I repeat, gentlemen"—growing a little warm at seeing a cursed grin breaking out round me—"as to a room's being haunted, I have as little faith in such silly stories as anyone. But, since you put the matter home to me, I will say that I have met with something in my room strange and inexplicable to me." A shout of laughter. "Gentlemen, I am serious. I know well what I am saying. I am calm, gentlemen." Striking my hand flat upon the table. "By heaven I am calm. I am neither trifling, nor do I wish to be trifled with." The laughter of the company suppressed with ludicrous attempts at gravity. "There is a picture in the room in which I was put last night that has had an effect upon me the most singular and incomprehensible."

"A picture!" said the old gentleman with the haunted head.

"A picture!" cried the narrator with the waggish nose.

"A picture! A picture!" echoed several voices. Here there was an ungovernable peal of laughter.

I could not contain myself. I started up from my seat—

looked round on the company with fiery indignation—thrust both my hands into my pockets, and strode up to one of the windows, as though I would have walked through it. I stopped short; looked out upon the landscape without distinguishing a feature of it; and felt my gorge rising almost to suffocation.

Mine host saw it was time to interfere. He had maintained an air of gravity through the whole of the scene, and now stepped forth as if to shelter me from the overwhelming merriment of my companions.

"Gentlemen," said he, "I dislike to spoil sport, but you have had your laugh, and the joke of the haunted chamber has been enjoyed. I must now take the part of my guest. I must not only vindicate him from your pleasantries, but I must reconcile him to himself, for I suspect he is a little out of humor with his own feelings; and above all, I must crave his pardon for having made him the subject of a kind of experiment.

"Yes, gentlemen, there is something strange and peculiar in the chamber to which our friend was shown last night. There is a picture which possesses a singular and mysterious influence; and with which there is connected a very curious story. It is a picture to which I attach a value from a variety of circumstances; and though I have often been tempted to destroy it from the odd and uncomfortable sensations it produces in everyone that beholds it, yet I have never been able to prevail upon myself to make the sacrifice. It is a picture I never like to look upon myself; and which is held in awe by all my servants. I have, therefore, banished it to a room but rarely used; and should have had it covered last night, had not the nature of our conversation, and the whimsical talk about a haunted chamber tempted me to let it remain, by way of experiment, whether a stranger, totally unacquainted with its story, would be affected by it."

The words of the baronet had turned every thought into a different channel. All were anxious to hear the story of the mysterious picture; and for myself, so strongly were my feelings interested that I forgot to feel piqued at the experiment which my host had made upon my nerves, and joined eagerly in the general entreaty.

As the morning was stormy, and precluded all egress, my host was glad of any means of entertaining his company; so drawing his armchair beside the fire, he began—

THE ADVENTURE OF THE MYSTERIOUS STRANGER

MANY YEARS SINCE, WHEN I WAS A young man, and had just left Oxford, I was sent on the grand tour to finish my education. I believe my parents had tried in vain to inoculate me with wisdom; so they sent me to mingle with society, in hopes I might take it the natural way. Such, at least, appears to be the reason for which nine tenths of our youngsters are sent abroad.

In the course of my tour I remained some time at Venice. The romantic character of the place delighted me; I was very much amused by the air of adventure and intrigue that prevailed in this region of masks and gondolas; and I was exceedingly smitten by a pair of languishing black eyes that played upon my heart from under an Italian mantle. So I persuaded myself that I was lingering at Venice to study men and manners. At least I persuaded my friends so, and that answered all my purpose. Indeed, I was a little prone to be struck by peculiarities in character and conduct, and my imagination was so full of romantic associations with Italy that I was always on the lookout for adventure.

Everything chimed in with such a humor in this old mermaid of a city. My suite of apartments was in a proud, melancholy palace on the grand canal, formerly the residence of a magnifico, and sumptuous with the traces of decayed grandeur. My gondolier was one of the shrewdest of his class, active, merry, intelligent, and, like his brethren, as secret as the grave; that is to say, secret to all the world except his master. I had not had him a week before he put me behind all the curtains in Venice. I liked the silence and mystery of the place, and when I sometimes saw from my window a black gondola gliding mysteriously along in the dusk of the evening, with nothing visible but its little glimmering lantern, I would jump into my own zenduletto and give a signal for pursuit.

"But I am running away from my subject with the recollection of youthful follies," said the baronet, checking himself. "Let me come to the point."

Among my familiar resorts was a casino under the arcades on one side of the grand square of Saint Mark. Here I used frequently to lounge and take my ice on those warm summer nights when in Italy everybody lives abroad until morning. I was seated here one evening, when a group of Italians took seat at a table on the opposite side of the saloon. Their conversation was happy and animated, and carried on with Italian vivacity and gesticulation.

I remarked among them one young man, however, who appeared to take no share, and find no enjoyment in the conversation; though he seemed to force himself to attend to it. He was tall and slender, and of extremely prepossessing appearance. His features were fine, though emaciated. He had a profusion of black glossy hair that curled lightly about his head, and contrasted with the extreme paleness of his countenance. His brow was haggard; deep furrows seemed to have been plowed into his visage by care, not by age, for he was evidently in the prime of youth. His eyes were full of expression and fire, but wild and unsteady. He seemed to be tormented by some strange fancy or apprehension. In spite of every effort to fix his attention on the conversation of his companions, I noticed that every now and then he would turn his head slowly round, give a glance over his shoulder, and then withdraw it with a sudden jerk, as if something painful had met his eye. This was repeated at intervals of about a minute, and he appeared hardly to have gotten over one shock before I saw him slowly preparing to encounter another.

After sitting some time in the casino, the party paid for the refreshments they had taken, and departed. The young man was the last to leave the saloon, and I remarked him glancing behind him in the same way, just as he passed out at the door. I could not resist the impulse to rise and follow him; for I was at an age when a romantic feeling of curiosity is easily awakened. The party walked slowly down the arcades, talking and laughing as they went. They crossed the piazzetta, but paused in the middle of it to enjoy the scene. It was one of those moonlit nights so brilliant and clear in the pure atmosphere of Italy. The moonbeams streamed onto the tall tower of Saint Mark, and lighted up the magnificent front and swelling domes of the cathedral. The party expressed their delight in animated terms. I kept my eye upon the young man. He alone seemed abstracted and self-occupied. I noticed the same singular, and, as it were, furtive glance over the shoulder that had attracted my attention in the casino. The party moved on, and I followed; they passed along the walks called the Broglio; turned the corner of the ducal palace, and, getting into a gondola, glided swiftly away.

The countenance and conduct of this young man dwelled upon my mind. There was something in his appearance that interested me exceedingly. I met him a day or two after in a gallery of paintings. He was evidently a connoisseur, for he always singled out the most masterly productions, and the few remarks drawn from him by his companions showed an intimate acquaintance with the art. His own taste, however, ran on singular extremes. On Salvator Rosa in his most savage and solitary scenes; on Raphael, Titian, and Correggio in their softest delineations of female beauty. On these he would occasionally gaze with transient enthusiasm. But this seemed only a momentary forgetfulness. Still would recur that cautious glance behind, and always quickly withdrawn, as though something terrible had met his view.

I encountered him frequently afterwards. At the theater, at balls, at concerts; at the promenades in the gardens of San Giorgio; at the grotesque exhibitions in the square of Saint Mark; among the throng of merchants on the exchange by the Rialto. He seemed, in fact, to seek crowds; to hunt after bustle and amusement; yet never to take any interest in either the business or gaiety of the scene. Ever an air of painful thought, of wretched abstraction; and ever that strange and recurring movement, of glancing fearfully over the shoulder. I did not know at first but this might be caused by apprehension of arrest; or perhaps from dread of assassination. But, if so, why should he go thus continually abroad; why expose himself at all times and in all places?

I became anxious to know this stranger. I was drawn to him by that romantic sympathy that sometimes draws young men towards each other. His melancholy threw a charm about him in my eyes, which was no doubt heightened by the touching expression of his countenance, and the manly graces of his person; for manly beauty has its effect even upon man. I had an Englishman's habitual diffidence and awkwardness of address to contend with; but I subdued it, and from frequently meeting him in the casino, gradually edged myself into his acquaintance. I had no reserve on his part to contend with. He seemed on the contrary to court society; and in fact to seek anything rather than be alone.

When he found I really took an interest in him, he threw himself entirely upon my friendship. He clung to me like a drowning man. He would walk with me for hours up and down the place of Saint Mark—or he would sit until night was far advanced in my apartment; he took rooms under the same roof with me; and his constant request was that I would permit him, when it did not incommode me, to sit by me in my saloon. It was not that he seemed to take a particular delight in my conversation; but rather that he craved the vicinity of a human being; and above all, of a being that sympathized with him.

"I have often heard," said he, "of the sincerity of Englishmen—thank God I have one at length for a friend!"

Yet he never seemed disposed to avail himself of my sympathy other than by mere companionship. He never sought to unlink himself from me; there appeared to be a settled corroding anguish in him that neither could be soothed "by silence nor by speaking." A devouring melancholy preyed upon his heart, and seemed to be drying up the very blood in his veins. It was not a soft melancholy—the disease of the affections—but a parching, withering agony. I could see at times that his mouth was dry and feverish; he almost panted rather than breathed; his eyes were bloodshot; his cheeks pale and livid; with now and then faint streaks athwart them— baleful gleams of the fire that was consuming his heart. As my arm was within his, I felt him press it at times with a convulsive motion to his side; his hands would clinch themselves involuntarily, and a kind of shudder would run through his frame. I reasoned with him about his melancholy, and sought to draw from him the cause—he shrunk from all confiding.

"Do not seek to know it," said he. "You could not relieve it if you knew it; you would not even seek to relieve it—on the contrary, I should lose your sympathy; and that," said he, pressing my hand convulsively, "that I feel has become too dear to me to risk."

I endeavored to awaken hope within him. He was young; life had a thousand pleasures in store for him; there is a healthy reaction in the youthful heart; it medicines its own wounds.

"Come, come," said I, "there is no grief so great that youth cannot outgrow it."

"No! No!" said he, clenching his teeth, and striking repeatedly, with the energy of despair, upon his chest. "It is here—here—deep-rooted; draining my heart's blood. It grows and grows, while my heart withers and withers! I have a dreadful monitor that gives me no repose—that follows me step-by-step; and will follow me step-by-step, until it pushes me into my grave!"

As he said this, he gave involuntarily one of those fearful glances over his shoulder, and shrank back with more than usual horror. I could not resist the temptation to allude to this movement, which I supposed to be some mere malady of the nerves. The moment I mentioned it, his face became crimsoned and convulsed—he grasped me by both hands.

"For God's sake," exclaimed he with a piercing agony of voice, "never allude to that again; let us avoid this subject, my friend; you cannot relieve me, indeed you cannot relieve me; but you may add to the torments I suffer. At some future day you shall know all."

I never resumed the subject; for however much my curiosity might be aroused, I felt too true compassion for his sufferings to increase them by my intrusion. I sought various ways to divert his mind, and to arouse him from the constant meditations in which he was plunged. He saw my efforts, and seconded them as far as in his power, for there was nothing moody or wayward in his nature; on the contrary, there was something frank, generous, unassuming, in his whole deportment. All the sentiments that he uttered were noble and lofty. He claimed no indulgence; he asked no toleration.

He seemed content to carry his load of misery in silence, and only sought to carry it by my side. There was a mute beseeching manner about him, as if he craved companionship as a charitable boon; and a tacit thankfulness in his looks, as if he felt grateful to me for not repulsing him.

I felt this melancholy to be infectious. It stole over my spirits; interfered with all my lively pursuits, and gradually saddened my life; yet I could not prevail upon myself to shake off a being who seemed to hang upon me for support. In truth, the generous traits of character that beamed through all this gloom had penetrated to my heart. His bounty was lavish and openhanded. His charity melting and spontaneous. Not confined to mere donations, which often humiliate as much as they relieve. The tone of his voice, the beam of his eye, enhanced every gift, and surprised the poor suppliant with that rarest and sweetest of charities, the charity not merely of the hand but of the heart. Indeed, his liberality seemed to have something in it of self-abasement and expiation. He humbled himself, in a manner, before the mendicant.

"What right have I to ease and affluence," would he murmur to himself, "when innocence wanders in misery and rags?"

The carnival time arrived. I had hoped that the joyful scenes which then presented themselves might have some cheering effect. I mingled with him in the motley throng that crowded the place of Saint Mark. We frequented operas, masquerades, balls. All in vain. The evil kept growing on him; he became more and more haggard and agitated. Often, after we had returned from one of these scenes of revelry, I entered his room, and found him lying on his face on the sofa: his hands clenched in his fine hair, and his whole countenance bearing traces of the convulsions of his mind.

The carnival passed away; the season of Lent succeeded; Passion Week arrived. We attended one evening a solemn service in one of the churches; in the course of which a grand piece of vocal and instrumental music was performed relating to the death of our Savior.

I had remarked that he was always powerfully affected by music; on this occasion he was so in an extraordinary degree. As the pealing notes swelled through the lofty aisles, he seemed to kindle up with fervor. His eyes rolled upwards, until nothing but the whites were visible; his hands were clasped together, until the fingers were deeply imprinted in the flesh. When the music expressed the dying agony, his face gradually sank upon his knees; and at the touching words resounding through the church, "Jesu mori," sobs burst from him uncontrolled. I had never seen him weep before; his had always been agony rather than sorrow. I augured well from the circumstance. I let him weep on uninterrupted. When the service was ended, we left the church. He hung on my arm as we walked homewards, with something of a softer and more subdued manner, instead of that nervous agitation I had been accustomed to witness. He alluded to the service we had heard.

"Music," said he, "is indeed the voice of heaven; never before have I felt more impressed by the story of the atonement of our Savior. Yes, my friend," said he, clasping his hands with a kind of transport, "I know that my Redeemer liveth."

We parted for the night. His room was not far from mine, and I heard him for some time busied in it. I fell asleep, but was awakened before daylight. The young man stood by my bedside, dressed for traveling. He held a sealed packet and a large parcel in his hand, which he laid on the table.

"Farewell, my friend," said he. "I am about to set forth on a long journey; but, before I go, I leave with you these remembrances. In this packet you will find the particulars of my story. When you read them, I shall be far away; do not remember me with aversion. You have been, indeed, a friend to me. You have poured oil into a broken heart, but you could not heal it. Farewell—let me kiss your hand—I am unworthy to embrace you." He sank to his knees, seized my hand in despite of my efforts to the contrary, and covered it with kisses. I was so surprised by all this scene that I had not been able to say a word.

"But we shall meet again," said I hastily as I saw him hurrying towards the door.

"Never—never in this world!" said he solemnly.

He sprang once more to my bedside—seized my hand, pressed it to his heart and to his lips, and rushed out of the room.

Here the baronet paused. He seemed lost in thought, and sat looking upon the floor and drumming with his fingers on the arm of his chair.

"And did this mysterious personage return?" said the inquisitive gentleman.

"Never!" replied the baronet, with a pensive shake of the head. "I never saw him again."

"And pray what has all this to do with the picture?" inquired the old gentleman with the nose.

"True!" said the questioner. "Is it the portrait of this crack-brained Italian?"

"No!" said the baronet dryly, not half liking the appellation given to his hero. "But this picture was enclosed in the parcel he left with me. The sealed packet contained its explanation. There was a request on the outside that I would not open it until six months had elapsed. I kept my promise, in spite of my curiosity. I have a translation of it by me, and had meant to read it, by way of accounting for the mystery of the chamber, but I fear I have already detained the company too long."

Here there was a general wish expressed to have the manuscript read; particularly on the part of the inquisitive gentleman. So the worthy baronet drew out a fairly written manuscript, and wiping his spectacles, read aloud the following story:

THE STORY OF THE YOUNG ITALIAN

I WAS BORN AT NAPLES. MY PARENTS, THOUGH of noble rank, were limited in fortune, or rather my father was ostentatious beyond his means, and expended so much in his palace, his equipage, and his retinue that he was continually straitened in his pecuniary circumstances. I was a younger son, and was looked upon with indifference by my father, who, from a principle of family pride, wished to leave all his property to my elder brother.

I showed, when quite a child, an extreme sensibility.

Everything affected me violently. While yet an infant in my mother's arms, and before I had learned to talk, I could be wrought upon to a wonderful degree of anguish or delight by the power of music. As I grew older, my feelings remained equally acute, and I was easily transported into paroxysms of pleasure or rage. It was the amusement of my relatives and of the domestics to play upon this irritable temperament. I was moved to tears, tickled to laughter, provoked to fury, for the entertainment of company, who were amused by such a tempest of mighty passion in a pygmy frame. They little thought, or perhaps little heeded the dangerous sensibilities they were fostering. I thus became a little creature of passion, before reason was developed. In a short time I grew too old to be a plaything, and then I became a torment. The tricks and passions I had been teased into became irksome, and I was disliked by my teachers for the very lessons they had taught me.

My mother died; and my power as a spoiled child was at an end. There was no longer any necessity to humor or tolerate me, for there was nothing to be gained by it, as I was no favorite of my father. I therefore experienced the fate of a spoiled child in such a situation, and was neglected, or noticed only to be crossed and contradicted. Such was the early treatment of a heart, which, if I am judge of it at all, was naturally disposed to the extremes of tenderness and affection.

My father, as I have already said, never liked me—in fact,

he never understood me; he looked upon me as willful and wayward, as deficient in natural affection. It was the stateliness of his own manner; the loftiness and grandeur of his own look that had repelled me from his arms. I always pictured him to myself as I had seen him clad in his senatorial robes, rustling with pomp and pride. The magnificence of his person had daunted my strong imagination. I could never approach him with the confiding affection of a child.

My father's feelings were wrapped up in my elder brother. He was to be the inheritor of the family title and the family dignity, and everything was sacrificed to him—I, as well as everything else. It was determined to devote me to the church, that so my humors and myself might be removed out of the way, either of tasking my father's time and trouble, or interfering with the interests of my brother. At an early age, therefore, before my mind had dawned upon the world and its delights, or known anything of it beyond the precincts of my father's palace, I was sent to a convent, the superior of which was my uncle, and I was confided entirely to his care.

My uncle was a man totally estranged from the world; he had never relished, for he had never tasted, its pleasures; and he deemed rigid self-denial as the great basis of Christian virtue. He considered everyone's temperament like his own; or at least he made them conform to it. His character and habits had an influence over the fraternity of which he was superior. A more gloomy, saturnine set of beings were never assembled together. The convent, too, was calculated to awaken sad and solitary thoughts. It was situated in a gloomy gorge of those mountains away south of Vesuvius. All distant views were shut out by sterile volcanic heights. A mountain stream raved beneath its walls, and eagles screamed about its turrets.

I had been sent to this place at so tender an age as soon to lose all distinct recollection of the scenes I had left behind. As my mind expanded, therefore, it formed its idea of the world from the convent and its vicinity, and a dreary world it appeared to me. An early tinge of melancholy was thus infused into my character; and the dismal stories of the monks, about devils and evil spirits, with which they affrighted my young imagination, gave me a tendency to superstition, which I could never effectually shake off. They took the same delight to work upon my ardent feelings that had been so mischievously exercised by my father's household.

I can recollect the horrors with which they fed my heated fancy during an eruption of Vesuvius. We were distant from that volcano, with mountains between us; but its convulsive throes shook the solid foundations of nature. Earthquakes threatened to topple down our convent towers. A lurid, baleful light hung in the heavens at night, and showers of ashes, borne by the wind, fell in our narrow valley. The monks talked of the earth being honey-combed beneath us; of streams of molten lava raging through its veins; of caverns of sulfurous flames roaring in the center, the abodes of demons and the damned; of fiery gulfs ready to yawn beneath our feet. All these tales were told to the doleful accompaniment of the mountain's thunders, whose low bellowing made the walls of our convent vibrate.

One of the monks had been a painter, but had retired from the world, and embraced this dismal life in expiation of some crime. He was a melancholy man, who pursued his art in the solitude of his cell, but made it a source of penance to him. His employment was to portray, either on canvas or in waxen models, the human face and human form, in the agonies of death and in all the stages of dissolution and decay. The fearful mysteries of the charnel house were unfolded in his labors—the loathsome banquet of the beetle and the worm. I turn with shuddering even from the recollection of his works. Yet, at that time, my strong but ill-directed imagination seized with ardor upon his instructions in his art. Anything was a variety from the dry studies and monotonous duties of the cloister. In a little while I became expert with my pencil, and my gloomy productions were thought worthy of decorating some of the altars of the chapel.

In this dismal way was a creature of feeling and fancy brought up. Everything genial and amiable in my nature was repressed and nothing brought out but what was unprofitable and ungracious. I was ardent in my temperament; quick, mercurial, impetuous, formed to be a creature of all love and adoration; but a leaden hand was laid on all my finer qualities. I was taught nothing but fear and hatred. I hated my uncle, I hated the monks, I hated the convent in which I was immured. I hated the world, and I almost hated myself, for being, as I supposed, so hating and hateful an animal.

When I had nearly attained the age of sixteen, I was suffered, on one occasion, to accompany one of the brethren on a mission to a distant part of the country. We soon left behind us the gloomy valley in which I had been pent up for so many years, and after a short journey among the mountains, emerged upon the voluptuous landscape that spreads itself about the Bay of Naples. Heavens! How transported was I, when I stretched my gaze over a vast reach of delicious sunny country, happy with groves and vineyards; with Vesuvius rearing its forked summit to my right; the blue Mediterranean to my left, with its enchanting coast, studded with shining towns and sumptuous villas; and Naples, my native Naples, gleaming far, far in the distance.

Good God! Was this the lovely world from which I had been excluded! I had reached that age when the sensibilities are in all their bloom and freshness. Mine had been checked and chilled. They now burst forth with the suddenness of a retarded spring. My heart, hitherto unnaturally shrunk up, expanded into a riot of vague but delicious emotions. The beauty of nature intoxicated, bewildered me. The song of the peasants; their cheerful looks; their happy avocations;

the picturesque gaiety of their dresses; their rustic music; their dances; all broke upon me like witchcraft. My soul responded to the music; my heart danced in my chest. All the men appeared amiable, all the women lovely.

I returned to the convent—that is to say, my body returned but my heart and soul never entered there again. I could not forget this glimpse of a beautiful and a happy world; a world so suited to my natural character. I had felt so happy while in it; so different a being from what I felt myself while in the convent—that tomb of the living. I contrasted the countenances of the beings I had seen, full of fire and freshness and enjoyment, with the pallid, leaden, lackluster visages of the monks; the music of the dance, with the droning chant of the chapel. I had before found the exercises of the cloister wearisome; they now became intolerable. The dull round of duties wore away my spirit; my nerves became irritated by the fretful tinkling of the convent bell; evermore dinging among the mountain echoes; evermore calling me from my repose at night, my pencil by day, to attend to some tedious and mechanical ceremony of devotion.

I was not of a nature to meditate long, without putting my thoughts into action. My spirit had been suddenly aroused, and was now all awake within me. I watched my opportunity, fled from the convent, and made my way on foot to Naples. As I entered its lively and crowded streets, and beheld the variety and stir of life around me, the luxury of palaces, the splendor of equipages, and the pantomimic animation of the motley populace, I seemed as if awakened to a world of enchantment, and solemnly vowed that nothing should force me back to the monotony of the cloister.

I had to inquire my way to my father's palace, for I had been so young on leaving it that I knew not its situation. I found some difficulty in getting admitted to my father's presence, for the domestics scarcely knew that there was such a being as myself in existence, and my monastic dress did not operate in my favor. Even my father entertained no recollection of my person. I told him my name, threw myself at his feet, implored his forgiveness, and entreated that I might not be sent back to the convent.

He received me with the condescension of a patron rather than the kindness of a parent. He listened patiently, but coldly, to my tale of monastic grievances and disgusts, and promised to think what else could be done for me. This coldness blighted and drove back all the frank affection of my nature that was ready to spring forth at the least warmth of parental kindness. All my early feelings towards my father revived; I again looked up to him as the stately magnificent being that had daunted my childish imagination, and felt as if I had no pretensions to his sympathies. My brother engrossed all his care and love; he inherited his nature, and carried himself towards me with a protecting rather than a fraternal air. It wounded my pride, which was great. I could brook condescension from my father, for I looked up to him with awe as a superior being, but I could not brook patronage from a brother, who, I felt, was intellectually my inferior. The servants perceived that I was an unwelcome intruder in the paternal mansion, and, menial-like, they treated me with neglect. Thus baffled at every point; my affections outraged wherever they would attach themselves, I became sullen, silent, and despondent. My feelings, driven back upon myself, entered and preyed upon my own heart. I remained for some days an unwelcome guest rather than a restored son in my father's house. I was doomed never to be properly known there. I was made, by wrong treatment, strange even to myself; and they judged of me from my strangeness.

I was startled one day at the sight of one of the monks of my convent, gliding out of my father's room. He saw me, but pretended not to notice me; and this very hypocrisy made me suspect something. I had become sore and susceptible in my feelings; everything inflicted a wound on them. In this state of mind I was treated with marked disrespect by a pampered minion, the favorite servant of my father. All the pride and passion of my nature rose in an instant, and I struck him to the earth.

My father was passing by; he stopped not to inquire the reason, nor indeed could he read the long course of mental sufferings which were the real cause. He rebuked me with anger and scorn; he summoned all the haughtiness of his nature, and grandeur of his look, to give weight to the contumely with which he treated me. I felt I had not deserved it—I felt that I was not appreciated—I felt that I had that within me which merited better treatment; my heart swelled against a father's injustice. I broke through my habitual awe of him. I replied to him with impatience; my hot spirit flushed in my cheek and kindled in my eye, but my sensitive heart swelled as quickly, and before I had half vented my passion, I felt it suffocated and quenched in my tears. My father was astonished and incensed at this turning of the worm, and ordered me to my chamber. I retired in silence, choking with contending emotions.

I had not been long there when I overheard voices in an adjoining apartment. It was a consultation between my father and the monk, about the means of getting me back quietly to the convent. My resolution was taken. I had no longer a home nor a father. That very night I left the paternal roof. I got on board a vessel making sail from the harbor, and abandoned myself to the wide world. No matter to what port she steered; any part of so beautiful a world was better than my convent. No matter where I was cast by fortune; any place would be more a home to me than the home I had left behind. The vessel was bound to Genoa. We arrived there after a voyage of a few days.

As I entered the harbor, between the moles which embrace it, and beheld the amphitheater of palaces and churches and splendid gardens, rising one above another, I felt at once its title to the appellation of Genoa the Superb. I landed on the mole an utter stranger, without knowing what to do, or whither to direct my steps. No matter; I was released from the thralldom of the convent and the humiliations of home! When I traversed the Strada Balbi and the Strada Nuova, those streets of palaces, and gazed at the wonders of architecture around me; when I wandered at close of day, amid a happy throng of the brilliant and the beautiful, through the green alleys of the Acqua Verdi, or among the colonnades and terraces of the magnificent Doria gardens, I thought it impossible to be ever otherwise than happy in Genoa.

A few days sufficed to show me my mistake. My scanty purse was exhausted, and for the first time in my life I experienced the sordid distress of penury. I had never known the want of money, and had never adverted to the possibility of such an evil. I was ignorant of the world and all its ways; and when first the idea of destitution came over my mind, its effect was withering. I was wandering pensively through the streets which no longer delighted my eyes, when chance led my stops into the magnificent church of the Annunziata.

A celebrated painter of the day was at that moment superintending the placing of one of his pictures over an altar. The proficiency which I had acquired in his art during my residence in the convent had made me an enthusiastic amateur. I was struck, at the first glance, by the painting. It was the face of a Madonna. So innocent, so lovely, such a divine expression of maternal tenderness! I lost for the moment all recollection of myself in the enthusiasm of my art. I clasped my hands together, and uttered an ejaculation of delight. The painter perceived my emotion. He was flattered and gratified by it. My air and manner pleased him, and he accosted me. I felt too much the want of friendship to repel the advances of a stranger, and there was something in this one so benevolent and winning that in a moment he gained my confidence.

I told him my story and my situation, concealing only my name and rank. He appeared strongly interested by my recital; invited me to his house, and from that time I became his favorite pupil. He thought he perceived in me extraordinary talents for the art, and his encomiums awakened all my ardor. What a blissful period of my existence was it that I passed beneath his roof. Another being seemed created within me, or rather, all that was amiable and excellent was drawn out. I was as recluse as ever I had been at the convent, but how different was my seclusion. My time was spent in storing my mind with lofty and poetical ideas; in meditating on all that was striking and noble in history or fiction; in studying and tracing all that was sublime and beautiful in nature. I was always a visionary, imaginative being, but now my reveries and imaginings all elevated me to rapture.

I looked up to my master as to a benevolent genius that had opened to me a region of enchantment. I became devotedly attached to him. He was not a native of Genoa, but had been drawn thither by the solicitation of several of the nobility, and had resided there but a few years, for the completion of certain works he had undertaken. His health was delicate, and he had to confide much of the filling up of his designs to the pencils of his scholars. He considered me as particularly happy in delineating the human countenance; in seizing upon characteristic, though fleeting, expressions and fixing them powerfully upon my canvas. I was employed continually, therefore, in sketching faces, and often when some particular grace or beauty or expression was wanted in a countenance, it was entrusted to my pencil. My benefactor was fond of bringing me forward; and partly, perhaps, through my actual skill, and partly by his partial praises, I began to be noted for the expression of my countenances.

Among the various works which he had undertaken was a historical piece for one of the palaces of Genoa, in which were to be introduced the likenesses of several of the family. Among these was one entrusted to my pencil. It was that of a girl, who as yet was in a convent for her education. She came out for the purpose of sitting for the picture. I first saw her in an apartment of one of the sumptuous palaces of Genoa. She stood before a casement that looked out upon the bay; a stream of vernal sunshine fell upon her, and shed a kind of glory round her as it lit up the rich crimson chamber. She was but sixteen years of age—and oh, how lovely! The scene broke upon me like a mere vision of spring and youth and beauty. I could have fallen down and worshipped her. She was like one of those fictions of poets and painters, when they would express the beau ideal that haunts their minds with shapes of indescribable perfection.

I was permitted to sketch her countenance in various positions, and I fondly protracted the study that was undoing me. The more I gazed on her, the more I became enamored; there was something almost painful in my intense admiration. I was but nineteen years of age; shy, diffident, and inexperienced. I was treated with attention and encouragement, for my youth and my enthusiasm in my art had won favor for me; and I am inclined to think that there was something in my air and manner that inspired interest and respect. Still the kindness with which I was treated could not dispel the embarrassment into which my own imagination threw me when in presence of this lovely being. It elevated her into something almost more than mortal. She seemed too exquisite for earthly use; too delicate and exalted for human attainment. As I sat tracing her charms on my canvas, with my eyes occasionally riveted on her features, I drank in delicious poison that made me giddy. My heart alternately gushed with tenderness and ached with despair. Now I became more than ever sensible of the violent fires that had lain dormant at the bottom of my soul. You who are born in a more temperate climate and under a cooler sky have little idea of the violence of passion in our southern areas.

A few days finished my task; Bianca returned to her convent, but her image remained indelibly impressed upon my heart. It dwelled on my imagination; it became my pervading idea of beauty. It had an effect even upon my pencil; I became noted for my felicity in depicting female loveliness; it was but because I multiplied the image of Bianca. I soothed, and yet fed, my fancy, by introducing her into all the productions of my master. I have stood with delight in one of the chapels of the Annunziata, and heard the crowd extol the seraphic beauty of a saint which I had painted; I have seen them bow down in adoration before the painting: they were bowing before the loveliness of Bianca.

I existed in this kind of dream, I might almost say delirium, for upwards of a year. Such is the tenacity of my imagination that the image which was formed in it continued in all its power and freshness. Indeed, I was a solitary, meditative being, much given to reverie, and apt to foster ideas which had once taken strong possession of me. I was roused from this fond, melancholy, delicious dream by the death of my worthy benefactor. I cannot describe the pangs his death occasioned me. It left me alone and almost brokenhearted. He bequeathed to me his little property; which, from the liberality of his disposition and his expensive style of living, was indeed but small; and he most particularly recommended me, in dying, to the protection of a nobleman who had been his patron.

The latter was a man who passed for munificent. He was a lover and an encourager of the arts, and evidently wished to be thought so. He fancied he saw in me indications of future excellence; my pencil had already attracted attention; he took me at once under his protection; seeing that I was overwhelmed with grief, and incapable of exerting myself in the mansion of my late benefactor, he invited me to sojourn for a time in a villa which he possessed on the border of the sea, in the picturesque neighborhood of Sestri Ponente.

I found at the villa the count's only son, Filippo: he was nearly of my age, prepossessing in his appearance, and fascinating in his manners; he attached himself to me, and seemed to court my good opinion. I thought there was something of profession in his kindness, and of caprice in his disposition; but I had nothing else near me to attach myself to, and my heart felt the need of something to repose itself upon. His education had been neglected; he looked upon me as his superior in mental powers and acquirements, and tacitly acknowledged my superiority. I felt that I was his equal in birth, and that gave an independence to my manner which had its effect. The caprice and tyranny I saw sometimes exercised on others, over whom he had power, were never manifested towards me. We became intimate friends, and frequent companions. Still I loved to be alone, and to indulge in the reveries of my own imagination, among the beautiful scenery by which I was surrounded.

The villa stood in the midst of ornamented grounds, finely decorated with statues and fountains, and laid out into groves and alleys and shady bowers. It commanded a wide view of the Mediterranean, and the picturesque Ligurian coast. Everything was assembled here that could gratify the taste or agreeably occupy the mind. Soothed by the tranquility of this elegant retreat, the turbulence of my feelings gradually subsided, and, blending with the romantic spell that still reigned over my imagination, produced a soft voluptuous melancholy.

I had not been long under the roof of the count when our solitude was enlivened by another inhabitant. It was a daughter of a relation of the count, who had lately died in reduced circumstances, bequeathing this only child to his protection. I had heard much of her beauty from Filippo, but my fancy had become so engrossed by one idea of beauty as not to admit of any other. We were in the central saloon of the villa when she arrived. She was still in mourning, and approached, leaning on the count's arm. As they ascended the marble portico, I was struck by the elegance of her figure and movement, by the grace with which the mezzaro, the bewitching veil of Genoa, was folded about her slender form.

They entered. Heavens! What was my surprise when I beheld Bianca before me. It was herself; pale with grief; but still more matured in loveliness than when I had last beheld her. The time that had elapsed had developed the graces of her person; and the sorrow she had undergone had diffused over her countenance an irresistible tenderness.

She blushed and trembled at seeing me, and tears rushed into her eyes, for she remembered in whose company she had been accustomed to behold me. For my part, I cannot express what were my emotions. By degrees I overcame the extreme shyness that had formerly paralyzed me in her presence. We were drawn together by sympathy of situation. We had each lost our best friend in the world; we were each, in some measure, thrown upon the kindness of others. When I came to know her intellectually, all my ideal picturings of her were confirmed. Her newness to the world, her delightful susceptibility to everything beautiful and agreeable in nature, reminded me of my own emotions when first I escaped from the convent. Her rectitude of thinking delighted my judgment; the sweetness of her nature wrapped itself around my heart; and then her young and tender and budding loveliness sent a delicious madness to my brain.

I gazed upon her with a kind of idolatry, as something more than mortal; and I felt humiliated at the idea of my comparative unworthiness. Yet she was mortal; and one of mortality's most susceptible and loving compounds; for she loved me!

How first I discovered the transporting truth I cannot recollect; I believe it stole upon me by degrees, as a wonder past hope or belief. We were both at such a tender and loving age; in constant interaction with each other; mingling in the same elegant pursuits; for music, poetry, and painting were our mutual delights, and we were almost separated from society, among lovely and romantic scenery! Is it strange that two young hearts thus brought together should readily twine round each other?

Oh, gods! What a dream—a transient dream—of unalloyed delight then passed over my soul! Then it was that the world around me was indeed a paradise, for I had a woman—lovely, delicious woman, to share it with me. How often have I rambled over the picturesque shores of Sestri, or climbed its wild mountains, with the coast gemmed with villas, and the blue sea far below me, and the slender Pharo of Genoa on its romantic promontory in the distance; and as I sustained the faltering steps of Bianca, have thought no unhappiness could enter into so beautiful a world. Why, oh, why is this budding season of life and love so transient—why is this rosy cloud of love that sheds such a glow over the morning of our days so prone to brew up into the whirlwind and the storm!

I was the first to awaken from this blissful delirium of the affections. I had gained Bianca's heart. What was I to do with it? I had no wealth nor prospects to entitle me to her hand. Was I to take advantage of her ignorance of the world, of her confiding affection, and draw her down to my own poverty? Was this requiting the hospitality of the count? Was this requiting the love of Bianca?

Now first I began to feel that even successful love may have its bitterness. A corroding care gathered about my heart. I moved about the palace like a guilty being. I felt as if I had abused its hospitality—as if I were a thief within its walls. I could no longer look with unembarrassed mien on the countenance of the count. I accused myself of perfidy to him, and I thought he read it in my looks, and began to distrust and despise me. His manner had always been ostentatious and condescending; it now appeared cold and haughty. Filippo, too, became reserved and distant; or at least I suspected him to be so. Heavens! Was this mere coinage of my brain? Was I to become suspicious of all the world—a poor surmising wretch; watching looks and gestures; and torturing myself with misconstructions? Or if true—was I to remain beneath a roof where I was merely tolerated, and linger there on sufferance?

"This is not to be endured!" exclaimed I. "I will tear myself from this state of self-abasement; I will break through this fascination and fly. Fly? Wither? From the world? For where is the world when I leave Bianca behind me?"

My spirit was naturally proud, and swelled within me at the idea of being looked upon with contumely. Many times I was on the point of declaring my family and rank, and asserting my equality, in the presence of Bianca, when I thought her relatives assumed an air of superiority. But the feeling was transient. I considered myself discarded and contemned by my family; and had solemnly vowed never to own relationship to them, until they themselves should claim it.

The struggle of my mind preyed upon my happiness and my health. It seemed as if the uncertainty of being loved would be less intolerable than thus to be assured of it, and yet not dare to enjoy the conviction. I was no longer the enraptured admirer of Bianca; I no longer hung in ecstasy on the tones of her voice, nor drank in with insatiate gaze the beauty of her countenance. Her very smiles ceased to delight me, for I felt culpable in having won them.

She could not but be sensible of the change in me, and inquired the cause with her usual frankness and simplicity. I could not evade the inquiry, for my heart was full to aching. I told her all the conflict of my soul; my devouring passion, my bitter self-upbraiding.

"Yes!" said I. "I am unworthy of you. I am an offcast from my family—a wanderer—a nameless, homeless wanderer, with nothing but poverty for my portion, and yet I have dared to love you—have dared to aspire to your love!"

My agitation moved her to tears; but she saw nothing in my situation so hopeless as I had depicted it. Brought up in a convent, she knew nothing of the world, its wants, its cares—and, indeed, what woman is a worldly casuist in matters of the heart! Nay, more—she kindled into a sweet enthusiasm when she spoke of my fortunes and myself. We had dwelled together on the works of the famous masters.

I had related to her their histories; the high reputation, the influence, the magnificence to which they had attained—the companions of princes, the favorites of kings, the pride and boast of nations. All this she applied to me. Her love saw nothing in their greatest productions that I was not able to achieve; and when I saw the lovely creature glow with fervor, and her whole countenance radiant with the visions of my glory, which seemed breaking upon her, I was snatched up for the moment into the heaven of her own imagination.

I am dwelling too long upon this part of my story; yet I cannot help lingering over a period of my life on which, with all its cares and conflicts, I look back with fondness; for as yet my soul was unstained by a crime. I do not know what might have been the result of this struggle between pride, delicacy, and passion, had I not read in a Neapolitan gazette an account of the sudden death of my brother. It was accompanied by an earnest inquiry for intelligence concerning me, and a prayer, should this notice meet my eye, that I would hasten to Naples, to comfort an infirm and afflicted father.

I was naturally of an affectionate disposition; but my brother had never been as a brother to me; I had long considered myself as disconnected from him, and his death caused me but little emotion. The thoughts of my father, infirm and suffering, touched me, however, to the quick; and when I thought of him, that lofty, magnificent being, now bowed down and desolate, and suing to me for comfort, all my resentment for past neglect was subdued, and a glow of filial affection was awakened within me.

The predominant feeling, however, that overpowered all others was transport at the sudden change in my whole fortunes. A home—a name—a rank—wealth awaited me; and love painted a still more rapturous prospect in the distance. I hastened to Bianca, and threw myself at her feet.

"Oh, Bianca," exclaimed I, "at length I can claim you for my own. I am no longer a nameless adventurer, a neglected, rejected outcast. Look—read, behold the tidings that restore me to my name and to myself!"

I will not dwell on the scene that ensued. Bianca rejoiced in the reverse of my situation, because she saw it lightened my heart of a load of care; for her own part she had loved me for myself, and had never doubted that my own merits would command both fame and fortune.

I now felt all my native pride buoyant within me; I no longer walked with my eyes bent to the dust; hope elevated them to the skies; my soul was lit up with fresh fires, and beamed from my countenance.

I wished to impart the change in my circumstances to the count; to let him know who and what I was, and to make formal proposals for the hand of Bianca; but the count was absent on a distant estate. I opened my whole soul to Filippo. Now first I told him of my passion; of the doubts and fears that had distracted me, and of the tidings that had suddenly dispelled them. He overwhelmed me with congratulations and with the warmest expressions of sympathy. I embraced him in the fullness of my heart. I felt compunctious for having suspected him of coldness, and asked him forgiveness for having ever doubted his friendship.

Nothing is so warm and enthusiastic as a sudden expansion of the heart between young men. Filippo entered into our concerns with the most eager interest. He was our confidant and counselor. It was determined that I should hasten at once to Naples to re-establish myself in my father's affections and my paternal home, and the moment the reconciliation was effected and my father's consent ensured, I should return and demand Bianca of the count. Filippo engaged to secure his father's acquiescence; indeed, he undertook to watch over our interests, and was the channel through which we were to correspond.

My parting with Bianca was tender—delicious—agonizing. It was in a little pavilion of the garden which had been one of our favorite resorts. How often and often did I return to have one more adieu—to have her look once more on me in speechless emotion—to enjoy once more the rapturous sight of those tears streaming down her lovely cheeks—to seize once more on that delicate hand, the frankly accorded pledge of love, and cover it with tears and kisses! Heavens! There is a delight even in the parting agony of two lovers worth a thousand tame pleasures of the world. I have her at this moment before my eyes—at the window of the pavilion, putting aside the vines that clustered about the casement—her light form beaming forth in virgin white—her countenance all tears and smiles—sending a thousand and a thousand adieus after me, as, hesitating, in a delirium of fondness and agitation, I faltered my way down the avenue.

As the bark bore me out of the harbor of Genoa, how eagerly my eyes stretched along the coast of Sestri, till it discerned the villa gleaming from among trees at the foot of the mountain. As long as day lasted, I gazed and gazed upon it, till it lessened and lessened to a mere white speck in the distance; and still my intense and fixed gaze discerned it, when all other objects of the coast had blended into indistinct confusion, or were lost in the evening gloom.

On arriving at Naples, I hastened to my paternal home. My heart yearned for the long-withheld blessing of a father's love. As I entered the proud portal of the ancestral palace, my emotions were so great that I could not speak. No one knew me. The servants gazed at me with curiosity and surprise. A few years of intellectual elevation and development had made a prodigious change in the poor fugitive stripling from the convent. Still, that no one should know me in my rightful home was overpowering. I felt like the prodigal son returned. I was a stranger in the house of my father. I burst into tears, and wept aloud. When I made myself known, however, all was changed. I who had once been almost repulsed from its walls, and forced to fly as an exile, was welcomed back with acclamation, with servility. One of the servants hastened to prepare my father for my reception; my eagerness to receive the paternal embrace was so great that I could not await the servant's return but hurried after him.

What a spectacle met my eyes as I entered the chamber! My father, whom I had left in the pride of vigorous age, whose noble and majestic bearing had so awed my young imagination, was bowed down and withered into decrepitude. A paralysis had ravaged his stately form, and left it a shaking ruin. He sat propped up in his chair, with pale, relaxed visage and glassy, wandering eyes. His intellects had evidently shared in the ravage of his frame. The servant was endeavoring to make him comprehend the visitor that was at hand. I tottered up to him and sank at his feet. All his past coldness and neglect were forgotten in his present sufferings. I remembered only that he was my parent, and that I had deserted him. I clasped his knees; my voice was almost stifled with convulsive sobs.

"Pardon—pardon—oh my father!" was all that I could utter.

His apprehension seemed slowly to return to him. He gazed at me for some moments with a vague, inquiring look; a convulsive tremor quivered about his lips; he feebly extended a shaking hand, laid it upon my head, and burst into an infantine flow of tears.

From that moment he would scarcely spare me from his sight. I appeared the only object that his heart responded to in the world; all else was as a blank to him. He had almost lost the powers of speech, and the reasoning faculty seemed at an end. He was mute and passive; excepting that fits of childlike weeping would sometimes come over him without any immediate cause. If I left the room at any time, his eye was incessantly fixed on the door till my return, and on my entrance there was another gush of tears.

To talk with him of my concerns, in this ruined state of mind, would have been worse than useless; to have left him, for ever so short a time, would have been cruel, unnatural. Here then was a new trial for my affections. I wrote to Bianca an account of my return and of my actual situation; painting in colors vivid, for they were true, the torments I suffered at our being thus separated; for to the youthful lover, every day of absence is an age of love lost. I enclosed the letter in one to Filippo, who was the channel of our correspondence. I received a reply from him full of friendship and sympathy; from Bianca full of assurances of affection and constancy.

Week after week, month after month elapsed, without making any change in my circumstances. The vital flame, which had seemed nearly extinct when first I met my father, kept fluttering on without any apparent diminution. I watched him constantly, faithfully—I had almost said patiently. I knew that his death alone would set me free; yet

I never at any moment wished it. I felt too glad to be able to make any atonement for past disobedience; and, denied as I had been all endearments of relationship in my early days, my heart yearned towards a father, who, in his age and helplessness, had thrown himself entirely on me for comfort. My passion for Bianca gained daily more force from absence; by constant meditation it wore itself a deeper and deeper channel. I made no new friends nor acquaintances; sought none of the pleasures of Naples which my rank and fortune threw open to me. Mine was a heart that confined itself to few objects, but dwelled upon those with the intenser passion. To sit by my father, and administer to his wants, and to meditate on Bianca in the silence of his chamber, was my constant habit. Sometimes I amused myself with my pencil in portraying the image that was ever present to my imagination. I transferred to canvas every look and smile of hers that dwelled in my heart. I showed them to my father in hopes of awakening an interest in his chest for the mere shadow of my love; but he was too far sunk in intellect to take any more than a childlike notice of them.

When I received a letter from Bianca, it was a new source of solitary luxury. Her letters, it is true, were less and less frequent, but they were always full of assurances of unabated affection. They breathed not the frank and innocent warmth with which she expressed herself in conversation, but I accounted for it from the embarrassment which inexperienced minds have often to express themselves upon paper. Filippo assured me of her unaltered constancy. They both lamented in the strongest terms our continued separation, though they did justice to the filial feeling that kept me by my father's side.

Nearly eighteen months elapsed in this protracted exile. To me they were so many ages. Ardent and impetuous by nature, I scarcely know how I should have supported so long an absence, had I not felt assured that the faith of Bianca was equal to my own. At length my father died. Life went from him almost imperceptibly. I hung over him in mute affliction, and watched the expiring spasms of nature. His last faltering accents whispered repeatedly a blessing on me—alas! How has it been fulfilled!

When I had paid due honors to his remains, and laid them in the tomb of our ancestors, I arranged briefly my affairs; put them in a posture to be easily at my command from a distance, and embarked once more, with a bounding heart, for Genoa.

Our voyage was propitious, and oh, what was my rapture when first, in the dawn of morning, I saw the shadowy summits of the Apennines rising almost like clouds above the horizon. The sweet breath of summer just moved us over the long wavering billows that were rolling us on towards Genoa. By degrees the coast of Sestri rose like a sweet creation of enchantment from the silver of the deep. I beheld the line of villages and palaces studding its borders.

My eye reverted to a well-known point, and at length, from the confusion of distant objects, it singled out the villa which contained Bianca. It was a mere speck in the landscape, but glimmering from afar, the polestar of my heart.

Again I gazed at it for a livelong summer's day; but oh how different the emotions between departure and return. It now kept growing and growing, instead of lessening on my sight. My heart seemed to dilate with it. I looked at it through a telescope. I gradually defined one feature after another. The balconies of the central saloon where first I met Bianca beneath its roof; the terrace where we so often had passed the delightful summer evenings; the awning that shaded her chamber window—I almost fancied I saw her form beneath it. Could she but know her lover was in the bark whose white sail now gleamed on the sunny area of the sea! My fond impatience increased as we neared the coast. The ship seemed to lag lazily over the billows; I could almost have sprung into the sea and swam to the desired shore.

The shadows of evening gradually shrouded the scene, but the moon arose in all her fullness and beauty and shed the tender light so dear to lovers, over the romantic coast of Sestri. My whole soul was bathed in unutterable tenderness. I anticipated the heavenly evenings I should pass in wandering with Bianca by the light of that blessed moon.

It was late at night before we entered the harbor. As early next morning as I could get released from the formalities of landing, I threw myself on horseback and hastened to the villa. As I galloped round the rocky promontory on which stands the Faro, and saw the coast of Sestri opening up on me, a thousand anxieties and doubts suddenly sprang up in my heart. There is something fearful in returning to those we love, while yet uncertain what ills or changes absence may have effected. The turbulence of my agitation shook my very frame. I spurred my horse to redoubled speed; he was covered with foam when we both arrived, panting, at the gateway that opened to the grounds around the villa. I left my horse at a cottage and walked through the grounds, that I might regain tranquility for the approaching interview. I chided myself for having suffered mere doubts and surmises thus suddenly to overcome me; but I was always prone to be carried away by these gusts of the feelings.

On entering the garden everything bore the same look as when I had left it; and this unchanged aspect of things reassured me. There were the alleys in which I had so often walked with Bianca; the same shades under which we had so often sat during the noontide. There were the same flowers of which she was fond; and which appeared still to be under the ministry of her hand. Everything around looked and breathed of Bianca; hope and joy flushed in my heart at every step. I passed a little bower in which we had often sat and read together. A book and a glove lay on the bench. It was Bianca's glove; it was a volume of the Metastasio I had given her. The glove lay in my favorite passage. I clasped them to my heart.

"All is safe!" exclaimed I, with rapture. "She loves me! She is still my own!"

I bounded lightly along the avenue down which I had faltered so slowly at my departure. I beheld her favorite pavilion which had witnessed our parting scene. The window was open, with the same vine clambering about it, precisely as when she waved and wept me an adieu. Oh! How transporting was the contrast in my situation. As I passed near the pavilion, I heard the tones of a female voice. They thrilled through me with an appeal to my heart not to be mistaken. Before I could think, I *felt* they were Bianca's. For an instant I paused, overpowered with agitation. I feared to break in suddenly upon her. I softly ascended the steps of the pavilion. The door was open. I saw Bianca seated at a table; her back was towards me; she was warbling a soft melancholy air, and was occupied in drawing. A glance sufficed to show me that she was copying one of my own paintings. I gazed on her for a moment in a delicious tumult of emotions. She paused in her singing; a heavy sigh, almost a sob followed. I could no longer contain myself.

"Bianca!" exclaimed I, in a half-smothered voice. She started at the sound; brushed back the ringlets that hung clustering about her face; darted a glance at me; uttered a piercing shriek, and would have fallen to the earth, had I not caught her in my arms.

"Bianca! My own Bianca!" exclaimed I, folding her to my chest; my voice stifled in sobs of convulsive joy. She lay in my arms without sense or motion. Alarmed at the effects of my own precipitation, I scarce knew what to do. I tried by a thousand endearing words to call her back to consciousness. She slowly recovered, and half opened her eyes.

"Where am I?" murmured she faintly.

"Here," exclaimed I, pressing her to my chest. "Here! Close to the heart that adores you; in the arms of your faithful Ottavio!"

"Oh no! No! No!" shrieked she, starting into sudden life and terror. "Away! Away! Leave me! Leave me!"

She tore herself from my arms; rushed to a corner of the saloon, and covered her face with her hands, as if the very sight of me were baleful. I was thunderstruck—I could not believe my senses. I followed her, trembling, confounded. I endeavored to take her hand, but she shrank from my very touch with horror.

"Good heavens, Bianca," exclaimed I, "what is the meaning of this? Is this my reception after so long an absence? Is this the love you professed for me?"

At the mention of love, a shuddering ran through her. She turned to me a face wild with anguish. "No more of that! No more of that!" gasped she. "Talk not to me of love. I—I—am married!"

I reeled as if I had received a mortal blow. A sickness struck to my very heart. I caught at a window frame for support. For a moment or two, everything was chaos around me. When I recovered, I beheld Bianca lying on a sofa; her face buried in a pillow, and sobbing convulsively. Indignation at her fickleness for a moment overpowered every other feeling.

"Faithless—perjured—" cried I, striding across the room. But another glance at that beautiful being in distress checked all my wrath. Anger could not dwell together with her idea in my soul.

"Oh, Bianca," exclaimed I in anguish, "could I have dreamed of this; could I have suspected you would have been false to me?"

She raised her face all streaming with tears, all disordered with emotion, and gave me one appealing look. "False to you! They told me you were dead!"

"What," said I, "in spite of our constant correspondence?"

She gazed wildly at me. "Correspondence! What correspondence?"

"Have you not repeatedly received and replied to my letters?"

She clasped her hands with solemnity and fervor. "As I hope for mercy, never!"

A horrible surmise shot through my brain. "Who told you I was dead?"

"It was reported that the ship in which you embarked for Naples perished at sea."

"But who told you the report?"

She paused for an instant, and trembled. "Filippo!"

"May the God of heaven curse him!" cried I, extending my clenched fists aloft.

"Oh, do not curse him—do not curse him!" exclaimed she. "He is—he is—my husband!"

This was all that was wanting to unfold the perfidy that had been practiced upon me. My blood boiled like liquid fire in my veins. I gasped with rage too great for utterance. I remained for a time bewildered by the whirl of horrible thoughts that rushed through my mind. The poor victim of deception before me thought it was with her I was incensed. She faintly murmured forth her exculpation. I will not dwell upon it. I saw in it more than she meant to reveal. I saw with a glance how both of us had been betrayed.

"'Tis well!" muttered I to myself in smothered accents of concentrated fury. "He shall account to me for this!"

Bianca overhead me. New terror flashed in her countenance. "For mercy's sake do not meet him—say nothing of what has passed—for my sake say nothing to him. I only shall be the sufferer!"

A new suspicion darted across my mind. "What!" exclaimed I. "Do you then *fear* him—is he *unkind* to you—tell me," reiterated I, grasping her hand and looking her eagerly in the face. "Tell me—*dares* he to use you harshly?"

"No! No! No!" cried she, faltering and embarrassed; but the glance at her face had told me volumes. I saw in her pallid and wasted features; in the prompt terror and subdued agony of her eyes a whole history of a mind broken down by tyranny. Great God! And was this beauteous flower snatched from me to be thus trampled upon? The idea roused me to madness. I clenched my teeth and my hands; I foamed at the mouth; every passion seemed to have resolved itself into the fury that like a lava boiled within my heart. Bianca shrank from me in speechless affright. As I strode by the window, my eye darted down the alley. Fatal moment! I beheld Filippo at a distance! My brain was in a delirium—I sprang from the pavilion, and was before him with the quickness of lightning. He saw me as I came rushing upon him—he turned pale, looked wildly to right and left, as if he would have fled, and, trembling, drew his sword.

"Wretch!" cried I. "Well may you draw your weapon!"

I spoke not another word—I snatched forth a stiletto, put by the sword which trembled in his hand, and buried my poniard in his chest. He fell with the blow, but my rage was unsated. I sprang upon him with the bloodthirsty feeling of a tiger; redoubled my blows; mangled him in my frenzy, grasped him by the throat, until with reiterated wounds and strangling convulsions he expired in my grasp. I remained glaring on the countenance, horrible in death, that seemed to stare back with its protruded eyes upon me. Piercing shrieks roused me from my delirium. I looked round and beheld Bianca flying distractedly towards us. My brain whirled. I waited not to meet her, but fled from the scene of horror. I fled forth from the garden like another Cain, a hell within my chest, and a curse upon my head. I fled without knowing whither—almost without knowing why. My only idea was to get farther and farther from the horrors I had left behind; as if I could throw space between myself and my conscience. I fled to the Apennines, and wandered for days and days among their savage heights. How I existed I cannot tell—what rocks and precipices I braved, and how I braved them, I know not. I kept on and on—trying to outtravel the curse that clung to me. Alas, the shrieks of Bianca rang forever in my ear. The horrible countenance of my victim was forever before my eyes. The blood of Filippo cried to me from the ground. Rocks, trees, and torrents all resounded with my crime.

Then it was I felt how much more insupportable is the anguish of remorse than every other mental pang. Oh! Could I but have cast off this crime that festered in my heart; could I but have regained the innocence that reigned in my breast as I entered the garden at Sestri; could I but have restored my victim to life, I felt as if I could look on with transport even though Bianca were in his arms.

By degrees this frenzied fever of remorse settled into a permanent malady of the mind. Into one of the most horrible that ever a poor wretch was cursed with. Wherever I went, the countenance of him I had slain appeared to follow me.

Wherever I turned my head, I beheld it behind me, hideous with the contortions of the dying moment. I have tried in every way to escape from this horrible phantom; but in vain. I know not whether it is an illusion of the mind, the consequence of my dismal education at the convent, or whether a phantom really sent by heaven to punish me; but there it ever is—at all times—in all places—nor has time nor habit had any effect in familiarizing me with its terrors. I have traveled from place to place, plunged into amusements—tried dissipation and distraction of every kind—all—all in vain.

I once had recourse to my pencil as a desperate experiment. I painted an exact resemblance of this phantom face. I placed it before me in hopes that by constantly contemplating the copy I might diminish the effect of the original. But I only doubled instead of diminishing the misery.

Such is the curse that has clung to my footsteps—that has made my life a burden—but the thoughts of death, terrible. God knows what I have suffered. What days and days, and nights and nights, of sleepless torment. What a never-dying worm has preyed upon my heart; what an unquenchable fire has burned within my brain. He knows the wrongs that wrought upon my poor weak nature; that converted the tenderest of affections into the deadliest of fury. He knows best whether a frail erring creature has expiated, by long-enduring torture and measureless remorse, the crime of a moment of madness. Often, often have I prostrated myself in the dust, and implored that he would give me a sign of his forgiveness, and let me die.—

Thus far had I written some time since. I had meant to leave this record of misery and crime with you, to be read when I should be no more. My prayer to heaven has at length been heard. You were witness to my emotions last evening at the performance of the Miserere; when the vaulted temple resounded with the words of atonement and redemption. I heard a voice speaking to me from the midst of the music; I heard it rising above the pealing of the organ and the voices of the choir; it spoke to me in tones of celestial melody; it promised mercy and forgiveness, but demanded from me full expiation. I go to make it. Tomorrow I shall be on my way to Genoa to surrender myself to justice. You who have pitied my sufferings; who have poured the balm of sympathy into my wounds, do not shrink from my memory with abhorrence now that you know my story. Recollect, when you read of my crime, I shall have atoned for it with my blood!

When the baronet had finished, there was a universal desire expressed to see the painting of this frightful visage. After much entreaty the baronet consented, on condition that they should only visit it one by one. He called his housekeeper and gave her charge to conduct the gentlemen singly to the chamber. They all returned varying in their stories: some affected in one way, some in another; some more, some less; but all agreeing that there was a certain something about the painting that had a very odd effect upon the feelings.

I stood in a deep bow window with the baronet, and could not help expressing my wonder. "After all," said I, "there are certain mysteries in our nature, certain inscrutable impulses and influences, that warrant one in being superstitious. Who can account for so many persons of different characters being thus strangely affected by a mere painting?"

"And especially when not one of them has seen it!" said the baronet with a smile.

"How?" exclaimed I. "Not seen it?"

"Not one of them?" replied he, laying his finger on his lips in sign of secrecy. "I saw that some of them were in a bantering vein, and I did not choose that the memento of the poor Italian should be made a jest of. So I gave the housekeeper a hint to show them all to a different chamber!"

Thus end the Stories of the Nervous Gentleman.